THE OLD MAN AND THE BENCH

Urs Allemann

Translated by Patrick Greaney

Champaign/London/Dublin

Originally published in German as
Urs Allemann, *Der alte Mann und die Bank:*
Ein Fünfmonatsgequassel (Vienna: Deuticke, 1993).

Library of Congress Cataloging-in-Publication Data
Allemann, Urs.
   [Alte Mann und die Bank. English]
   The old man and the bench / by Urs Allemann ;
   translated by Patrick Greaney. -- First edition.
     pages cm
   ISBN 978-1-62897-016-6 (pbk. : alk. paper)
   I. Greaney, Patrick, translator. II. Title.
   PT2661.L552A6813 2014
   833'.92--dc23
                                        2014029966

swiss arts council
prohelvetia

Partially funded by a grant by the Illinois Arts Council
Published in collaboration with the Swiss Arts Council
Pro Helvetia, Zurich

www.dalkeyarchive.com
Cover: design and composition by Mikhail Iliatov
Printed on permanent/durable and acid-free paper

THE OLD MAN AND THE BENCH

The Old Man and the Bench

It's that time. Finally. He's an old man. Today he's sitting on his bench. It's the first time. From now on he'll come here every day. It's his place of work. He'll reminisce about his childhood. For five months. The old man flinches. That's how it's said. Frightened that how it's said was said he flinches again. He didn't even bring his pocket mirror. Tomorrow then. It's too late today. It's not worth closing his eyes now. The old man goes home like he will every evening from now on. No one he claims ever said anything about a deadline.

He's sitting there again. He doesn't know yet if he should count his days. Yesterday. Today. The old man doesn't appear to be in a hurry. He's spent his life waiting for this moment. Now it's here. Now he'd rather wait a bit longer. His eyes are open. He just keeps on staring without seeing anything. If he closes them he knows the reminiscing will start right away. Not yet. Until the day before yesterday he was still alive. Now life's over. Childhood will be here any minute. Maybe he feels like taking a vacation on his bench.

The old man doesn't have a name. But he's not naked. He makes a point of saying that. If someone thinks he's naked that's their fault. His asphalt gray herringbone coat with the basalt gray buttons. His cement gray hat with a graphite gray silk ribbon thrown around it. The old man shakes his fists with rage at the chatter pitter-pattering down out of the blue out of his mouth into his ears. He prevails. It seems he's allowed to make small corrections. Gray herringbone coat gray hat gray shoes. Maybe a gray scarf. Maybe some gray earmuffs. Gray mouthmuffs handmuffs nosemuffs. Gray woolen nosemuff on to warm up his he shakes his fists again. Coat hat shoes scarf. Those are his things. Maybe a pair of socks. That's what he has on. That's what he wanted to say. He tries to imagine what the old man looks like. Stupid of him he doesn't have a pocket mirror today either.

It would never occur to anyone listening to the old man talking that somewhere in this world there's a bench the man's sitting on. But there it is. A wooden bench. Green. The bench is outside. A park bench. Unfortunately though there's no park. The old man checks his watch. To give himself some life signs he breathes in and out for half a minute loud enough to hear himself breathe in and out. Slowly. After twenty-eight seconds he knows he's breathed in four times and breathed out four times. To fill up the half minute the old man is faced with the choice of either continuing to breathe out by exerting pressure on his lungs for two seconds beyond the end of the exhalation's expiration beyond the end of the exhalation part of the breathing-out stage of the fourth breath unit of the total breathing process in the current breath modeling experiment or opening his mouth two seconds too soon and suckingslurpinggulpinggobbling up into his hole air that doesn't even belong to him. Problem solved but he doesn't say how. Too ashamed. He'd rather not be so totally transparent to himself so soon. He's not going to lose track anyway. If he would only decide to keep count today would be the third day. Time he stresses is not what he's short on.

Instead of reminiscing about his childhood he could describe the house that he leaves every morning that he returns to every evening. He won't he curses ever describe anything at all. But why not. Why doesn't he just stay in bed in the bedroom on the second floor and imagine that he's sitting at the kitchen table in the kitchen on the first floor writing something about the old man sitting outside on his bench reminiscing about his childhood. Most of the rooms in the house are empty. Not empty there's some furniture in there it's just the old man doesn't set foot in the rooms. Why doesn't he sit at the kitchen table and try here or get into bed and try there to reminisce about his childhood. Perhaps that's the way it'll be someday he says.

One morning he'll be too tired to get up from this
kitchen table and throw on this herringbone coat as
if he'd ever thrown it on put on this gray hat as if he'd
ever for the ten or five minutes it takes to go down
these streets through these woods no over these tram
tracks through this meadow along this creek alongside
this field or along anything else through anything over
anything to this bench or one morning he's too tired
to get out of this bed pull on this robe as if he'd to
descend these stairs into the kitchen or anywhere else
into the cellar oil cellar coal cellar he shakes his fists
one morning he'll be too tired to wake up in this bed
as if lachrymose blabbermouth he howls.

It's his house because it belongs to him. It's his prop-
erty. The old man lives there all alone. No one has
the right to dispute his right to the rooms he inhabits
the rooms he doesn't inhabit. It's his house it's his
bench. He sits on it all alone. It's his bench because
it's the same every day because he sits on it every day.
It doesn't belong to him. Everyone else has the same
right as he does to sit on this bench. But it always
seems to be unoccupied. Eight o'clock on the dot
every morning the old man is at his place of work.
It's never been taken. Never when he's gotten there
has anyone else been sitting on his bench. Never has
anyone else sat down on the bench while he's been
sitting there. Presumably there'd be room on the
bench for three. That's never been tried out. Every
evening five o'clock on the dot the old man leaves

his place of work. It's his house it's his bench it's his childhood.

Week two. The old man closes his eyes. Black square. Black rectangle black bar maybe. Be quiet look. Black surface. White dot on it. White dot is saying too much. There isn't anything to see yet. A tiny nick vanishing against the black where the black is a little less black. Black paint applied eon-thick a pinpoint of thinner black. A fingernail gets to work on the back of the picture and scrapes off the paper and one of the seven layers of black. Two of seven three of seven. The fingernail keeps scraping. Out of whose wart does it trickle into this hole. Constant dripping wears away the. A milk-black star shines in a tar-black sky. How is it that the black material has gotten threadbare in one spot. Come up with a story for this point. After eons away with the eons the eons is laying it on too thick. Once upon a time there was a black. Since it had always been black it believed it could count on staying black forever. Wrong. One day it got a gray speck that everted and turned into a gray pimple the next day. Maybe it's my redemption carbuncle grumbled the black exaltedly. The gray pimple didn't grow instead it grew lighter every day. When it turns white it'll fall off so prophesized the black and an immaculate black will appear underneath it. Wrong. When the pimple turned white the black got a second speck that everted and became a pimple the next day. Speck and pimple such was the progression were white from the outset.

The next day two new white pimples appeared on the black. The new pimples such was the progression were pimples from the outset. An hour later such was the progression four new white pimples appeared on the black that together with the four old white pimples such was the progression after a minute such was the progression began to grow. Within seconds the black lost all its illusions. The white pimples it shouted are growing together into megapimples. Now the giant white unified pimple is it shouted eating up the remaining black. Wrong. Forty-nine percent of the black was bepimpled white. Then all of a sudden the white pimple scab fell off. Immaculate black appeared underneath. So much for the carbuncle the black smirked melancholically. Fell asleep in a bad mood. And it lived happily blackly ever after that is if its dream didn't make it white. Or some other story. Like how the poor domino got numeric leprosy. The old man opens his eyes. Curses. Limps home.

Everything said about the old man the old man says himself. In many cases he might know what he's talking about. In other cases he doesn't.

He's sitting on the bench. He'd prefer for it to be a season. Autumn for instance. He says the word autumn but it doesn't help. If someone were to come by he imagines they'd see the word AUTUMN with six capital letters standing up straight in the old man's mouth. Wooden letters. My letters his letters. There's no shit too pretentious for that degenerate childish brain to shamelessly crap it out into the blabber potty. The inspired idea of having the letters first be green then yellow then brown and in November perhaps falling from the lips of the old man and gently drifting in the wind falling woefully wilted erratically to the ground is rejected without hesitation even by this autumnless twaddlemouth. Light blue he stammers and almost remembered something.

Fantasy. Language sweat gushes out of his every pore. Runs down over him flows together into a murky language stream. Swells up tears him along carries him along. Eyes closed. He can't swim he's just three years old. Does his underwater somersaults. Eyes open. There's the green bench. He just needs to stick his arm out of the surging water hold on tight pull himself ashore. That's how he got here. He takes his seat soaking wet. He'll dry out here. That takes time. He has he says more than enough time. It doesn't bother him that water's still dripping from his hat and coat. Calmly he watches as the water darkens the brown forest ground as it seeps into the pine needles. He closes his eyes. He'd like to reminisce without language about his childhood.

Pine needles. Wooden letters. Coal cellar. Somersaults in the water.

Prose. If some doesn't get finished he's finished.

The old man has to eat something. Everyone eats something. Him too. To say nothing of drinking well then why doesn't he just say nothing. Whoever sits on a bench for nine hours has to deal with hunger and thirst. It's not enough to indicate that every morning at the kitchen table he eats two pieces of crispbread. Without butter. He's never abhorred anything in his life as much as he abhors butter. Just soft smeary butter only soft smeary butter he never abhorred solid butter. To be spread all over his two crispbread pieces the butter would have to be soft and smeary. He would never succeed in spreading solid butter back and forth on the two pieces of crispbread instead of soft and smeary butter. The two crispbread pieces would fall apart on him under the knife. Crumbled up broken to pieces he would have a fit and smash the plate with the useless crispbread dust on the kitchen floor. Good thing it never occurred to the butter to do anything other than stay solid in which case he's not disgusted and sticks it back in the icebox or get soft and smeary in which case he's disgusted and throws it in the dustbin. Icebox dustbin since when has this geezer gone for local color antiquated lingo. Since when is this old man a geezer. Since when it's not enough to allude to the fact that he gets drunk every night in his kitchen. He never leaves the bottles he's finished on the kitchen table. Even when he's dead drunk he still knows that space on the kitchen table will be needed the next morning for the crispbread plate. Before bed he always carries the empty bottles over into the dining room that despite what he would have thought he sets foot in once a day for this purpose. He sets the bottles down on the dining room table. Once the table is full he's never calculated how long it takes to fill the table with bottles it's once again for the umpteenth time time for Winkelried the breaststroke swimmer. Short performance no audience. He stands up in front of the long side of the table bends down and stage 1 with his head tucked down between his shoulders with his hands held together to form a handpointer he advances with his arms into the sea of bottles. Space for hand arm head chest stomach must first be conquered. A few bottles fall over that's not worth mentioning. With his forehead pressed against the table surface he retools his useless hand pointer converts it into a double hand shovel by stage 2 turning his hands outwardsaway-fromoneanother towardseachother so that now his hand backs are touching instead of his hand bellies. Then he takes a breath then he raises up his head then stage 3 his left arm with the left hand shovel and his right arm with the right hand shovel simultaneously sweep clean the left half of the table the right half of the table the whole table surface. All the bottles are lying on the floor most of them shattered some of them unshattered. Along with tonight's bottles for whose sake the table surface has been swept clean. Exit Winkelried the breaststroke swimmer. No applause. But what does the old man eat what does he drink on his bench. No secret there. On the way from his house to the bench he makes a stop at the baker. Ten to eight sharp he buys three pretzels. The paper bag with the pretzels goes in his left coat pocket. The soda bottle he bought yesterday is sticking out of his right pocket. On the way home from the bench he makes a stop at the grocery store. At ten past five sharp he returns the soda bottle he finished that day and in exchange takes along the bottle he will finish the next day. Since the grocery store opens at eight in the morning and he has to be at his place of work at eight he always has to buy his soda the evening before. He doesn't return the paper bag to the baker. When he gets home in the evening before he gets drunk in the kitchen he throws the paper bag into the living room that despite what he would have thought he sets foot in once a day for this purpose. He sits on the bench chews the last piece of the pretzel gulps down the last of the soda screws the twist top onto the bottle screws the bottle cap onto the twist top screws the bottle cap that is perhaps called a twist top onto the bottle's bottle neck's bottle neck end's glass screw thread that might be called the twist top screws curses screws curses smoothes out the paper bag folds it sticks the paper bag in his left coat pocket the bottle in his right coat pocket stands up brushes the crumbs if there are crumbs off his coat goes home. Later on he'll get drunk in the kitchen. On beer oh yeah beer he can't get it in the grocery store from the baker sothenwheredoeshe.

The old man is offered a contract. Everything he says is treated as if it were on paper. Everything on paper is treated as if he said it. Excellent working conditions. Without thinking about what the contract might mean he accepts what he is offered by the old man.

Twaddles eyes closed twaddles eyes open twaddles.

His life. There's nothing to say about it. Having his childhood before him in his consciousness he quickly had it behind him. Five months is a long time. He no longer knows how long he's been living alone in the house.

It's hard to answer the question of whether the old man stinks. It's likely that he stinks but not enough to make himself nauseous. A restrained foul-smelling odor that complements the gray of his hat and coat. Anxiety alms ass abscess old ocular offal evening excretions. The old man is not of the opinion that of all the letters A O and E have the most disgusting smell. A homeowner is not going to get alms anyway. He is not at all of the opinion that sounds that letters are fragrant or stink. Whoever believes such a thing he yells should be he pauses pauses too briefly punched in the face. His tongue ripped out if he's talking his writing hand chopped off if he's writing. But why is he talking like that. He tries to shake his fists but doesn't succeed. Instead an involuntary wave of rage sends ripples down his back. Pathetic body tremolo. Man and bench as gray green yolk within the fragrance egg grayly sourly housing the yolk. As a yolk in a yolk.

Suddenly the wave ebbs away. The old man is busy creating order. Him the cock's treadle the bench the yolk foul smell egg white and shell. If someone were to get too close to him greet him lean over him still clueless sit down next to him if their nose were to break the shell they would become aware of the vaporous clouds of putrefaction rising up from the old man and hanging in the air around him. Creating order means recognizing that the first and innermost layer often called the kernel or empty coat is made up of gray flesh and the second and middle layer often called the skin or even wrapping paper is made up of the herringbone coat and in contrast the third and outermost layer often called the imperial husk or the celestial cloche is made up of the odor coating. Unfortunately the old man ascertains that what reaches his nostrils doesn't always remain the same. What smelled moderately foul yesterday smells immoderately foul today. Skepticism would be out of place here. The old man stinks. But creating order also means identifying the source of the stink. It's not the coat it's not the scarf it's not the old man's gloves shoes socks that stink. It's not the hat that stinks the stink emerges from under the hat. The old man's flesh stinks. His words stink. That's not the same thing. New questions emerge that are difficult to answer. Does the flesh stench recur in the words' stench. Does the word stench generate the flesh's stench. Would his flesh if the old man were mute stink less. Would the old man's words if he were fleshless stink even more. He eats his pretzel takes a gulp of soda. Wonders if he should think something up to fill up the empty coat. Ties his shoelaces tighter. Looks forward to his beer.

To the left of the bench there's a trashcan. To the right of the bench and behind the bench there are bushes. Unfortunately the old man has not been granted a tree. Alder he laments oak maple October. The rustling of the names of the tree of the names of the month. Cloudssunfograinwind. Dew and no dew. The first frosts. Hoarfrost. He's not sure. Crows jackdaws. If he has to pee he steps behind the bench and does it in the bushes. But who wants to know that. In front of the bench there's the path the bench is on. Beyond the path a field. Beyond the bushes begins the forest. The woods. He knows they wouldn't be woods if there weren't trees there. No consolation. No reason to turn around. The woods behind him don't make up for the linden tree the beech the walnut tree the chestnut.

All he has is language. That's why he hates it. Because he hates it he'll bite his tongue off. Some day. He says so.

Eyes closed. Black aquarium. There's only air no water. No glass no fish. Probably not even air. To figure out if there's air one would have to try to breathe. No one to be seen. Big like the coffin the bedroom the small universe. Birds chirping away no it's crickets chirping no it's more metallic than that. A hundred thousand nail scissors on the move in the aquarium. Impossible to follow the trail of their snipping. Impossible to describe the flight paths' curves and turns and loops. Nothing to be seen it can all just be heard. Good thing they aren't razor blades razor blades slice silently. It's the universe nothingness is in the universe the swarms of nail scissors scour the universe so they can snip every bit of nothingness to pieces. Be careful suddenly half an ear is gone. Imagine blood dripping into the aquarium. But two nail scissors never collide. There's quacking he's quacking. He's about to tell the story of the dueling nail scissors. Of how scissors A tries to cut up scissors B of how scissors B tries to cut up scissors A. Of how their steel jaws lock. From the snip bites and choke scrapes to the mute metal kiss snatched out of time. A draw. Nail scissor sheath on the night table. Dingy fraying triangular fake red leather flaps. Snaps shut. Ornamental fake black leather ribbon partly taken out of the seam partly snipped up by the tip of the nail scissors. Heel callus. Pubic hair. Out of the hole in the wall the wall trickles onto the floor. It's not necessary to turn the light on. It's not possible to get back into the aquarium again from the nursery. Is it possible is it necessary to demand of the old man that he decide between a hundred thousand invisible pairs of nail scissors and one single barely visible pair of nail scissors.

Variation. Not an aquarium but a block of wood. Giant black ashlar. A hundred thousand wood worms burrow their interlacing tunnels in it. They're not metal they're living worms. Not made of wood just eating wood. Feeding invisibly burrowing silently. No wood worm ticking to be heard. Time passes. The wood's hollowed out. The worms fatten up. Soon the worms will be compelled to eat even the wooden walls between the tube tunnels. If two worms meet the fatter worm eats the thinner worm. It's been agreed that the fatter one is also the stronger one. If the two worms are equally fat then usually it turns out that one of the two equally fat worms has gotten a bit fatter a bit faster than the other of the two once equally fat but now no longer equally fat worms. Once the fatter worm realizes it's now the fatter one it eats the worm that's now the thinner one in accordance with the law not caring whether or not the thinner worm realizes it's now the thinner one. Usually the fact that one worm has gotten a bit faster and a bit fatter than the other worm is due to the fact that one worm has spent its time eating wood while the other worm has wasted its time sleeping and taking a break from wood eating. Sometimes both worms grow equally fast. Then it's not long before a third worm happens upon the two of them and is fatter than both of them and therefore eats them in accordance with the law. It's been proven that worms that only eat wood grow more slowly than worms that eat wood and worms. Time passes. The wood's hollowed out. Barely any of it left. There are more fat worms but fewer worms as a whole. Barely any of them left. But the ones left are gigantic. At this point the old man starts dreaming of a spectacular finale. Two giant worms and the giant ashlar's thin wooden skin remain. Black casing. Contents two white worms that barely fit in there together. Two worms two strategies. One worm plans to eat the casing and thrust himself out of it. The other plans to eat the first worm and have the casing all to himself. Both of them begin to implement their plan. Just as the last piece of the casing disappears into worm 1 the last piece of worm 1 disappears into worm 2. Worm 2 whose plan unlike worm 1's never included thrusting itself out of the casing is now outside. However it's been robbed of the casing in which had it been alone it would have been comfortable. That he too would have one day been driven by hunger to eat the casing doesn't occur to him now. Too bad the worms weren't numbered inversely. Wouldn't it have been nicer if in the end instead of worm 2 worm 1 were alone in the world. Eyes open. What to do with the worm. Pick it up. Cuddle it. Throw it in the wastepaper basket. Put it in the freezer compartment in the icebox so he can work with it later.

Variations. Stone ashlar stone worms. Corpse ashlar corpse worms.

How old is he. He doesn't know. At the most 90 at least 65. He doesn't have to make a living anymore but he can still get it up. O he still gets it up he'll get him one day what was his profession before. Until he got old he claims he worked as a proofreader. For his whole life for money he made correct words out of incorrect words correct sentences out of incorrect sentences. On the weekend he buys himself two girls. At the newspaper stand at the tram stop he buys the newspaper with the numbers of girls willing to pay him a visit for money. It's not the newspaper he worked for as a proofreader it's the cheaper one. In the expensive newspaper he worked for as a proofreader there are the numbers of girls who would be willing to host him for money. The man doesn't buy the expensive newspaper. To be sure it would have been cheaper to pay a visit to girls who would be willing to host him for money than to host girls who are willing to pay him a visit for money. But the old man prefers to host visitors rather than to be hosted as a visitor. Why the old man marvels is the more expensive thing in the cheaper newspaper the cheaper thing in the more expensive newspaper. He marvels he doesn't get indignant. Since he's only been an old man for a few weeks he's probably 65 not 90. Unless he worked for the expensive newspaper as a proofreader until he was 90. With a monocle clamped in his half blind left eye he would have bent over so close to the paper with the words and sentences that his snow white hair would have flowed all over the words and sentences no longer in need of proofreading that his snow white beard hair would have flowed over the words and sentences still in need of proofreading. Thirty or fifty years ago it's said he shouts the old man wrote two books. He's

shaking with rage. Why he thinks about it does it have
to be two girls. Two isn't that a bit much one wouldn't
that be enough. At his age he's not going to get it up
twice. But then two if there are two might be enough
for each other. No need to talk to one of them when
each of them is already talking to the other one. As he
lies there in bed between them full of the knowledge
that tonight this night that joins Saturday and Sunday
he won't fall off the left side or the right side of the
bed the two of them are talking to each other over his
head. Did he already get it up did they already bring it
down he can't remember. Maybe when there are two
of them it's not necessary to get it up. Maybe they
tucked him in and they've rolled so close to each other
on top of the blanket they tucked him in with that
it's possible for them to suck on each other over him.
He doesn't even want to know what's in the books he
wrote back then. Should the old man he thinks about
it call the girls after he gets drunk in his kitchen like
he does every night. Or should he since he's going
to host the girls tonight not get drunk. Or should he
before he lets himself be brought to bed by the girls get
drunk in his kitchen with the girls. Should he maybe
offer the girls some beer. Should he before he gets
dragged by the girls dead drunk out of the kitchen
down the hall up the stairs into the bedroom bring
the empty bottles over into the dining room like he
does every other night. On Sunday morning should
he at the kitchen table offer the girls some crispbread
for the road. Will he be feeling stingy or generous.

Should he offer one or two pieces to each of them without butter with butter. Will he when the girls are gone spend his Sunday on the bench. Did he before the girls came spend his Saturday on the bench. How old is he. When and where does he pick up his pension. When and where his beer. Does he go out to the bench in every kind of weather.

Every sentence he says gags him he says and keeps him from saying the sentence he'd say if he weren't gagged. With every sentence that gags him he says the desire to say the other sentence that ungags him grows. There is the gagging sentence he says gagging himself there is the ungagging sentence. Every sentence as long as it hasn't been said promises to be the ungagging sentence but winds up as soon as it's been said he says gagging him. Speechless self-ungagging o he says there's a lot to say about that in the gagging sentence.

There's still no pocket mirror. But he does have a hand mirror on him. Brown. Oval. Wooden frame. Wooden handle. Much too big to precipitately pull it out of his coat pocket. If it were a tennis racket strung with glass he could pull it out of his gym bag. The story of the glass tennis match. Player A's serve. Player A throws the ball up prepares to strike hits it. The glass shatters. Advantage player B. Service change. Player B throws the ball up prepares to strike hits it. The glass shatters. Deuce. Service change. New rackets please. Player A

throws the ball up prepares to strike hits it. The glass
shatters. The game goes back and forth a draw. After
a few hours night falls. It doesn't have to be light out
for the glass to shatter. Maybe already that night but
definitely by the next day both players are wading knee
deep in shards of glass. What happens with the wood
cleared away by the wardens doesn't matter. Strung
with new glass it can be used again. Maybe already
the next day but definitely by the following night both
players bleed to death. Whoever bleeds to death last
wins. As prize and parting present the winner gets a
hand mirror that depending on whether he decides
on cremation or burial will be incinerated along with
him or placed in his coffin. What happens to the glass
in the case of the mirror's incineration doesn't matter.
Will it melt the old man is over his head on that one.
Ramrod straight he's sitting on his bench. Out of his
left hand the mirror sprouts ramrod straight. The
mirror and the old man form parallel lines and will
thus if everything ends well intersect at infinity. That
the arm is stuck out straight that the angle formed by
the arm and the man and by the arm and the mirror
are right angles in both cases is of course obvious. The
old man closes his eyes lowers his head. He simultaneously pulls his arm in thrusts his head out sticks
they meet. The glass shatters. Now the old man can
let go of the mirror it's hanging around his neck as if
it were a prize or a parting present. That would make
a nice photo but the photographer would have to be
quick because the old man pulls a pocket saw out of

his briefcase or out of his backpack that earlier he
pulled the pocket mirror out of and saws the useless
mirror frame off his neck. He throws the wood into
the trashcan sticks the pocket saw back in the briefcase and pulls a dustpan and hand broom out of the
backpack that earlier he pulled the pocket mirror and
pocket saw out of. Now just sweep up the glass and
dump it in the trashcan now just stick the dustpan
and brush back in the briefcase now just remember
tomorrow to finally bring the pocket mirror now just
eat another piece of pretzel have a gulp of soda brush
off the crumbs and now that's it for today time to go
home no first to the grocery.

Fantasy. He imagines an old man walking into a river
everyday. What kind of a river would that be a metaphorical one of course. And the old man who walks
into the river of course he too knows very well he's
just a metaphorical old man. But the point of the story
is that suddenly one day after weeks months or years
an actual old man walks out of the river shakes himself off sits himself down on the closest bench to dry
off a bit and claims that both of them the actual and
by the way pretty damn wet river over there and this
actual and by the way pretty damn old man right here
are what that howdidthatgoagain metaphorical and to
tell the truth pretty piddly mini-river piddling along
and that howdidthatgoagain metaphorical clapper trap
of an old man yammering away in a to tell the truth
pretty uninspired way were the okayokayokay damned

patient howdidthatgoagain metaphors for the whole
time. The old man looks surprised and doesn't believe
a word of what he says. But tomorrow he thinks and
thus says it too he will come up with something like
this again. It just annoys him that after all that time
and effort it turns out to be some asshole who walks
out of the river. That wasn't the plan.

He feels like trying out an experiment on himself.
Taking away his clothing taking away his language.
Locking himself in a cell without any clothing without any language. Through the peephole in the cell
door seeing how he without clothing without language
without seeing the eye in the peephole no seeing the
eye in the peephole no without seeing the eye no seeing the eye no without no he smashes his head against
the cell door. The eye in the peephole starts to rotate
which however the eye in the peephole can't see. Yes
it can. No it can't. Yes. No. The old man checks his
watch. The second critique. Maybe he wants to reminisce about his childhood because back then he didn't
yet have to take language away from himself. No one
ever said anything to him. He never said a thing.

Month two. Something has to change. Four months is
a long time. He'll have to force himself to remember
the canister with the white maggots. The container
with the black flies. But he knows that instead of
remembering the canister remembering the container
he'll wonder if there's a difference between the canister

and the container. Rounded. Aluminum. Aluminum alloy. Tin. Time for the magnet test. He gnashes his teeth he's strong enough not just to tremble but to shake his fists. To pit himself against the aluminum container the tin canister. Unless he gets crushed between the container and the canister. Between the container that's as big as a metal drum and weighs a ton and the canister that's as big as a metal drum and weighs a ton. He's lying in bed between the giant canister and the giant container that instead of sucking on each other over him speaking to one another over him roll over him and make him into a bloody flesh patty of an old man he closes his eyes he rolls out the cake batter covered in flour if it really is cake batter with the rolling pin with the roller the wooden rod has to be attached to the wooden handle through the wooden roller and the other wooden handle stuck onto the wooden rod stuck through the wooden roller then the rolling can begin then the flattening can begin then it's payback time for the batter time for the batter to pay for what he opens his eyes the container the canister will do to him if he doesn't manage to escape the canister the container he's not about to let himself be crushed by this container by this canister o he might be crushed if there were just one of them a canister a container but there are two of them a container and a canister the canister that would roll right over him if it were lying in bed with him alone bumps up against the container that would roll right over him if it were lying in bed with him alone but now bumps up against

the canister that would roll over him but now doesn't
roll over him because the canister is stopped by the
container that is stopped by the canister so that the
old man crawls out of the air pocket under the canister
under the container between container and canister he
shakes his fists he knows he has the strength to force
himself to remember the canister with the maggots
and the flies and if it was a container after all he knows
he has the strength to force himself to call the container a canister it was a canister it was booming and
roaring in there that was the flies the maggots couldn't
boom roar they were silent maggots silent fishermen
intended to catch silent fish with unless the silent fishermen intended to catch the silent fish with silenced
flies that had long ago stopped booming and roaring
suddenly the bait canister was partly open under the
lid half-dead half-alive flies were welling up in the
canister half-dead half-alive maggots were writhing
around it was the grandfather who opened the canister
the old man doesn't remember it being the grandfather
but he says it he says it could have been the grand he
could have been the grand he could be his own grandfather now he's twaddling on again he shakes his fists
he wipes the twaddle from his mouth with his right
with his left fist he knows he knew that half-dead flies
grew out of half-dead maggots that half-dead maggots
instead of dying all the way became half-dead flies he
could have imagined he said that half-alive flies infil-
trated the canister to feed on half-alive maggots to
become all the way alive by killing half-dead maggots

but he knows he knew he says that maggots are future flies and flies former maggots even if he didn't know doesn't know if the maggot's more disgusted that one day it'll be a fly or the fly's more disgusted that it was once a maggot or if the grandfather's more disgusted by the flies scuttling out of the maggot canister or by the maggots wriggling in the fly canister or if the grandson's more disgusted by the grandfather leaning over the maggots the flies or by the grandfather leaning over the grandfather's no the father's no the grandson's little prick or if the kid is more disgusted by the father leaning over the kid's no the father's little prick or by the mother leaning over the father's no the other kid's little prick or if the kid is more disgusted by the birth of the other kid or by his own birth or if the old man is more disgusted because he's had enough of always telling the story of his own birth.

Let him twaddle on he says. Be patient. Shake your fists be quiet. If he pours the twaddle through a sieve maybe the sieve will catch some twaddle clumps that the old man can think about on the bench. He doesn't have a sieve. He has to make one out of all the twaddle.

A trick. He's injured has to hide the injury from himself. So he starts bleeding simultaneously from five wounds. One real four invented wounds. The old man will never figure out which one is real. The real one heals beneath the herringbone coat. So it's an invented wound that gets infected. The old man dies. But this

death he says let them know he doesn't take his word
for it.

Bright November sun. A woman passes by on the path
the bench is on. The old man's eyes nearly pop out of
his head. Until a short while ago he never would've
thought something like this was possible. Wrinkles.
Half boots. Brown suede coat. Cloche hat. He doesn't
know what a cloche hat is but that shouldn't stop a
woman from wearing one. Creases. The old man lifts
his hat. The attempt to play the suave gentleman sitting in a rocking chair for the elderly drinking the
five-o'clock tea of life misfires. There's no role this
ham of an old man couldn't botch. He sticks out his
hat right in the woman's face bows like a cretin. She
rummages in her suede coat pocket looking for alms
finds a bonbon throws it in his hat. Bonbon's not a
problem he's familiar with the word familiar with
the object. Takes it out of his hat out of its wrapper
sticks it in his mouth smoothes out the wrapper folds
it twothree times puts it in his hat sticks his hat in
the woman's face. Two narrative threads. The bonbon
in his mouth the wrapper in his hat. It's a raspberry
bonbon that reminds him of a raspberry bonbon that
doesn't remind him of anything. The bonbon thread
the memory thread the childhood thread is a dead
end. The old man can't close his eyes focuses on the
wrapper in his hat. As implausible as it may seem the
woman in the meantime hasn't moved on. She stops
short takes the wrapper out of his hat sticks it without

unfolding it into her suede coat pocket says thank you. If this old man isn't a gentleman then maybe he has something else to offer. Throw the wrapper he says very quietly very slowly very clearly very menacingly very pointedly in the trashcan immediately. It's possible he thinks the woman has heard the word trashcan before but no longer knows or never knew what it meant. He puts his hat on reaches for his walking stick or cane that until now must have escaped his attention and points at the metal trashcan with the rubber tip that's there to dampen the rapping out of seconds on the sidewalk cement. The woman stops short rummages around in her suede coat pocket comes upon a coin throws it in the trashcan stops short rushes over to the trashcan digs around in the trashcan comes upon instead of the coin a roll a bun well preserved for its age holds it up for the old man stops short drops it flees. As implausible as it may seem the old man in the meantime has swallowed the bonbon whole instead of sucking on it till the end. Various possibilities for continuing the story. The old man limps after the woman so he can approach her violently tenderly or indifferently. The old man picks up the roll lying on the ground in front of him and sticks it in his mouth to punish it or the female stranger for something. The old man throws the bun in the trashcan digs around in the basket to find the coin but instead of the coin or the bun comes upon an old or new shattered or unshattered pocket mirror. The old man throws the roll in the trashcan fetches from the trashcan he doesn't

have to dig around for long the coin the woman she
regrets losing the coin comes back the old man hands
the coin to the woman the woman hands the folded
bonbon wrapper to the old man the old man spits the
bonbon out he didn't swallow it into his hat he raised
it for her wraps the bonbon in the bonbon wrapper
he unfolded it hands it to the woman she sticks it in
her suede coat pocket fumbles around in her suede
coat pocket comes upon a small white animal in the
suede coat pocket a little buffalo perhaps a little gnu
perhaps a tiny wild sow perhaps stops short plays for
a moment with the thought of taking the bonbon out
of the bonbon wrapper and sticking it in her mouth
and then swaddling the tiny dead wild sow in the bonbon wrapper and throwing it in the lousy old man's
greasy beggar hat what a face he would make when he
removed the wrapper from the tiny dead wild sow but
it's not the woman it's just the old man who played for
a moment with the thought of the face he would make
when he removed the wrapper from the tiny dead wild
sow while the woman without pulling anything out of
the suede coat pocket to throw in his hat like a frozen
Eskimo baby like a scalped Indio fetus like a shattered
test tube with a charred Negro embryo like a fertilized
but decomposed pygmy egg returned to where she
came from or somewhere else. No no. The old man
stays seated. Leans back. Pulls his hat down over his
forehead to protect himself from the November sun.
Looks down at the roll out of the corner of his half-
closed eye. As implausible as it may seem it's still lying

there. On the ground in front of him in the dirt. Not doing anything. Waiting for the ants.

The old man and the bench. He blows and blows. When he holds the gray balloon up against the light the bench and the old man don't escape his notice. While the bench appears to be a growth on the inside of the balloon skin the old man appears to be a growth on the bench skin. When he's blown it up enough the balloon and the old man who blew up the balloon and inexplicably the bench too on which the old man blew up the balloon will burst. That doesn't even matter. Because just at that moment the old man and the bench who and which in the meantime have expanded inside the balloon began to breathe. There's nothing comforting about that. Because inexplicably just at that moment a small gray balloon appeared that the old man naturally begins to blow up at once. The old man and the bench. He blows and blows. He already said that once. But back then he didn't want to tell the story that he then wound up telling. Instead he wanted to say that when he had blown enough one day a proper bench would be sitting there green and made of wood and on this bench there will sit a proper old man who maybe stinks a little but what does that matter and it's completely possible that the bench will be so rotten that it immediately collapses under the old man's weight that really doesn't carry any weight in this discussion and it's completely possible that the old man will be so tired that despite the fact that the bench just collapsed under him he will fall asleep most likely for good but what does that matter the main thing is this bench once existed the main thing is the old man once the main thing is the old man and the bench he blows and blows.

Bowel movement. Sometimes he craps water sometimes he craps rocks. The one thing he doesn't do is crap normally. That's how it's said. Where is he crapping. In the bushes. What does he wipe his behind with. Well who wants to know that. The color please. Gray rocks gray water. Be quiet.

The house. He's not done with the house. The bedroom with the square bed with room for three is right over the room that was once called the dining room. These days it's called the bottle room. The room that was once called the nursery is right over the kitchen. Over the paper bag room that was once called the living room there's another room. A woman used to live there. These days the old man burns his trash in there. Once a week once a month once a year. He's never calculated how long it takes to accumulate enough trash that it has to be burned. Crispbread packages crispbread crumbs paper napkins paper tissues notes. Notes to be burned no there aren't any of those lying around. It's contractually stipulated that he twaddle on about them on his bench. But couldn't he burn the twaddle instead of straining it. The story of the man who uses a Bunsen burner to singe from his lips the words with which a story might otherwise have been told. The blue Bunsen burner flame. Like the archangel Gabriel it patrols in front of his mouth. Darting flame punishing flame. Irresistible vengeful whoosh of the spirit. The old man's sitting in the theater or in the cinema. He's sitting in chemistry religion English class. Everything's black everything's quiet. Visible lips. Invisible inaudible words. Audible visible flame in front of his lips. The voice of the teacher in which the old man recognizes the voice of the old man explains that the flame is playing the role of the spirit consuming the decomposing flesh played by the words. The voice of the pupil in which the old man recognizes the voice of the old man asks if it might not be nicer if the words themselves leapt out of his mouth in the form of flames. Divine dragon spitting holy fiery language. The old man giggles and imagines the teacher and pupil going after each other with the Bunsen burners. While snot is blown into the paper tissues semen is shot into the paper napkins. The crispbread has already been discussed. When enough trash has built up the old man dumps it out on the round fire room table. He goes down into the cellar connects the garden hose in the laundry room. Rolling the garden hose out of the garden hose drum he goes back up to the second floor to the fire room. He opens the window hangs the garden hose over the windowsill. With a match he sets the trash on the table on fire. He goes down into the cellar turns the faucet on. Racing the water he goes back up the stairs he knows he can't win exerts himself as if he didn't know goes back upstairs to the second floor to the fire room. He hears the water shooting out the window sees the fire blazing away. Jerks the hose out of the window directs the stream towards the flames. He puts it out. He extinguishes the fire before the table that belonged to the woman who used to live in the room gets burnt. He closes the window goes down into the cellar turns the faucet off. He goes back up to the fire room drags the hose down into the cellar. Wet ashes wet ash-smeared stairway. To the left of the front door there's the powder room. Above the powder room and the front door there's the bathroom. It's at the other end of the hall at whose other end there's the room that's over the kitchen. If the old man wanted to light the house on fire but not himself he would throw a burning match into the paper bag room close the paper bag room door and exit the house through the front door. If the old man wanted to set the house and himself on fire he would throw a burning match into the paper bag room go up the stairs to the second floor sit down on the floor in the room over the kitchen wait.

He can't bear himself. Sentence without consequences.

He decided on the bench because he wanted to be outside. He's not outside.

Eyes closed. He hasn't been born yet. Eyes open. He's fallen on the tile floor.

If he had friends he would ask that they regard him as a piece of shit. O not just any old piece of shit though. He'd like to be the favorite piece. The little decayed gem locked away in a jewelry box during the week. Isn't our pitiful friend the loveliest among all the piles of shit so goes the exclamation of the friends gathered on Sunday to lean over the pile of shit on the velvet cushion. Because he's a pure flawless pile of shit and nothing but a pile of shit. A piece of shit that is to shit as cherry schnapps is to cherries. Cheers. A pile of shit the pile of shit the pile of shit par excellence. Never was shit so completely and totally shit as when it as when our friend appeared on this earth. The look on the old man's face lost dreamy his lips quivering. Why is he talking like that. He has no friends. Is this piece of shit he asks able to shut itself up in a jewelry box. To lock itself in. To gaze upon itself on Sundays he bellows he whispers to sniff itself.

Out of a hole in the bathroom ceiling a piece of shit fell onto the tile floor. His book. His first book. It occurred to him what was in it. He doesn't want to know will however tell himself once again what he already told himself back then once before without listening. Fecalstickbirthanddeath. Fecalstickselfreflection. He wants to force himself to listen. Doesn't want to listen to himself.

The old man feels like claiming that he reminisces about his childhood because he never had a childhood. That's the way it is he says. That's not the way it is. Gray flannel pants. Green velour jumper. No spankings. Rubber pants. Opapapapamamamamama. Swanskin.

Keep your mouth shut in the car. You'll get a coin for that. Blowing into the tonewood for a half hour. You'll get a coin for that. Making a wisecrack lashing himself in the face with the wisewhip impeccable slave dialectics he's not that little anymore he said that he can think of himself as big he's not that dumb anymore he said that he can think of himself as clever he's not that immature anymore he said that he when he gets a coin or something he buys someth. You'll get a coin for that.

Tonight when he gets home he'll lie down in the bathtub with his herringbone coat on. Lets go lets it flow. Before in the kitchen he wet be quiet. He doesn't turn any lights on. Dead drunk in his piss-wet herringbone coat he lies the night away in the tub dead drunk. In case he falls asleep he set the alarm. The second it rings he gets up and takes a shower in the herringbone coat. Then he dries himself in his herringbone coat with the blowdryer. He dries and dries. He put his hat on the toilet seat. Then he crawls on all fours through the bathroom door by the fire room door down the hall through the bedroom into his bed. Lets go lets it flow. Too weak to crawl back to the tub and shower again. Forgot his hat and the alarm clock in the bathroom. He'll still be right on time for crispbread the next morning. To get to the bench to. The herringbone coat seems to be stuck to the old man's skin encrusted on it. Might be grafted on. Can't take it off anymore. He'd if he tried to take it off bleed to death.

Maybe four men or four women are going to come over to beat him up. That's fine with him. As long as it doesn't hurt. They should give him a shot or knock him out with the laughing gas rag. When he wakes up he's lying in a pool of blood on the bench. No bones anymore. They packed them away in the potato sacks in the coal sacks. To the left of the front door there's the metal grate. Whoever lifts it up can send the coal the stuffed bear the stuffed tiger the stuffed leopard the bones tumbling down into the basement. Contained lunacy. He would like for his childhood to be beaten out of him by others. In his head he has four backs of heads walking away. He didn't get any further.

Book 1. The fecal stick. Grew out of the cave roof. Stuck itself out of the rock. Millimeter by millimeter it got older. Didn't see anything. Didn't know if there was nothing to see if it was dark or if the fecal stick was blind. Blind and mute. Without saying anything the fecal stick grew downwards. It grew milligram by milligram and didn't know whence it only knew that it was a fecal stick. Maybe it smelled that. Smelled its own smell. Became aware of fecal stick existence

as it became aware of the fecal stench. O it wasn't
the only fecal stick in the fecal stick cave. Hundreds
of thousands of fecal sticks grew from the cave roof
towards the floor. Didn't see one another. Said nothing.
Couldn't smell one another. Such was the degree to
which it was caught up in its own stench that it wasn't
even conscious of the stench of all the other fecal
sticks. Could be that the fecal stick was mistaken about
itself. Could be that the stench the fecal stick always
thought was its own was composed of its own and the
stench of other fecal sticks. The possibility of self-de-
ception was a thought the fecal stick could think. But
no matter what it thought it couldn't smell anything
except what was for it the stench. Its own. The one
and only. It was not able to differentiate stenches in the
stench. If it had smelled two stenches it would presumably have called one of them its own and the other one
the others'. The foreign one. But the fecal stick only
smelled one stench. Without smelling one another the
fecal sticks kept on growing alongside each other. Parallel to one another but o it's not going to end well.
Never will they meet in infinity since the cave floor
in all its finitude awaits them below. Growing cubic
centimeter by cubic centimeter not knowing whence
they knew they were not one they were hundreds of
thousands of fecal sticks. Pfffst. Maybe they heard it.
Pfffst. The fecal stick heard the fecal sticks falling.
Knew that the loud nearby pfffst and the distant quiet
pfffst pfffst was quiet were the pfffstpfffstpfffstpfffst
other fecal sticks hitting the cave floor. As it became

aware of the sound of the plopping fecal sticks the fecal
stick became aware of the end of fecal stick existence.
Pfffstop. The encounter of cave floor and fecal stick
it called death. The pushing of the fecal stick from
out of the cave roof this farewell that lasts an entire
fecal stick existence it called birth. Birth it explained
to itself is over when the fecal stick is finally so heavy
that it falls from the cave roof. Then it plummets to
the cave floor and dies. This plummet the moment of
the plummet the fecal stick called life. In the sudden
change from the all-too-slow growing on the rocks to
the all-too-fast plummeting onto the rocks it explained
to itself the fecal stick falls unconscious. Shock. The
one second of life is not experienced consciously. No
fecal stick experiences the life of a fecal stick. Gram
by gram decimeter by decimeter it grew older. Pfffst.
Pffpffpffst. The fecal stick hearkened the darkness.
Gave ear to the great fecal stick death music. It was
still conscious. It wasn't yet alive. It could still think
the thought that it would never hear the only sound it
would ever bring forth its own plop its dying plop its
death plop. It could still fear or hope that some other
fecal stick whose plop wouldn't precede but rather
follow its plop would be able to hear its first and only
plop as a tone as a differentiated particular tone in the
great fecal stick death music. It could still ask itself if it
was impossible to confuse one fecal stick's pfffst with
another fecal stick's pfffst or if it was in fact possible
to confuse them. Pfffst. It still had time to ponder
whether the pfffsts it heard everywhere could be dif-

ferentiated from one another only because sometimes
they were loud pfffsts and sometimes quiet ones which
it repeated to itself only meant that the fecal sticks
sometimes were pfffsting closer sometimes farther
away or if there was another difference between the
pfffsts and thus also between the fecal sticks whose
first and only pfffst whose death pfffst the pfffsts were.
It still had time to speculate that the dying sound of
the fecal stick may have been its name its death may
have been the fecal stick's christening. It kept getting
longer heavier older. Fell. Unconscious.

 The old man's not happy with the fecal stick story. He
clenches his fists lists off scornfully the objections. 1.
The story is not long enough to be a book. So if he's
written this story he hasn't written a book but if he's
written a book then he hasn't written this story. 2. Why
feces and not calcite. A sense of smell a smell isn't a
stalactite capable of having them. Why does the nar-
rator of this story lack such a belief. And it's not even
necessary that the fecal stick smell itself. Is the nar-
rator misusing the fecal stick to broadcast that he's a
pile of shit. 3. Where is time in this story. Why doesn't
time seize ensoul transform convulse purify the fecal
stick. 4. How does the fecal stick get away with con-
cluding that all the sounds in the dark are made by
beings just like it instead of just any old beings. Why
doesn't it say listenlisten it's sludging it's raining in
the cave the cave has diarrhea listenlisten wasn't that
a sound in the cave. 5. Didn't anyone think of the fact

that to the movement from above downwards there corresponds a movement from below upwards. That if a hundred thousand fecal sticks fall from the ceiling the feces level will rise. That where the cave once was soon there will be only feces. 6. The plop lie. Whoever calls the shattering of fecal sticks on a rock plopping is a liar.

Very last day of the second month. Weeks of rain. This morning's silent fog prelude this afternoon's November sun. On rainy days docs the old man wear a poncho over his herringbone coat. He laughs. He hadn't considered that. Difficulties dealing with the soda and pretzel bag. He squints. Never he says has he sat there so carefree on the green bench. What if someone were to ask him right now why the sun shines why he's there. No one actually asks him but he raises his hat to greet the flock of crows up above and the field over there. Even the fact that he doesn't know if they're really crows doesn't bother him today.

Can't he take off the herringbone coat. Can't he reminisce about his loved ones instead of about his childhood. Enter every room in his house for no reason. Look the woman the kid in the face who he says dissolved without a trace in the house in his head. Sadness. Fold up the green bench and put it in the trashcan. Go out. Strike up a conversation with a young woman. Chat with a friend over a cognac about the machinations of the powerful. Buy a suede coat a pair of corduroy pants. Fold up the trashcan and stick it in his pants' pocket. Gently bite the nape of the woman's neck or bite her senseless under her chin. Call the bottle room dining room the paper bag room living room. Burn the old man's loot make a library out of the fire room. Extinguish twenty thirty forty years. Write a sophisticatedly formulated politically lucid morally adept euphonic article against inhumanity. Whisper in the young woman's ear or lap something that he's sure will occur to him. Until the friend throws the cognac in his face drags the woman out of bed by her feet throws her over his shoulder and disappears with his booty into the mountain fog into another room somewhere anywhere. So that if it were to happen that way he would throw on his herringbone coat buy a dog crumble up the dog and throw the crumbs to the crows.

It's that time. Finally. He closes his eyes. The kid's at the door. In the room a piano's being played. It's a grand piano. The door's locked. The kid sees the woman's back. But wait that doesn't work. The kid leans his head up against the door. The word for this woman is mother he says. The old man knows his sentences don't go together. The woman he sees but whom the kid isn't able to see through the closed door but whom he sees is playing a Bach piano concerto. There's no way the kid could know that but the old man knows it. Piano concerto in D minor he says except that right now he can't think of the music. Doesn't matter he can just buy the record. Bought it years ago perhaps and hid it away somewhere in the basement or on the third floor of his house. The kid. He doesn't know if the kid has sensations. He sees the kid but wait that doesn't work. The kid's eyes grow out of the kid and see the kid standing in front of the door. So it's another kid he says but no he says that's not true. He's three or seven or might be three and seven. Maybe he's in front of one and then another door. In front of the wooden door in front of the frosted glass door. Simultaneously. The kid the woman the grand piano the music are still there. Unchanged. Only the door it's closed turned into another one. Maybe he says one door was locked but the other one wasn't. Suddenly both the old man's eyeballs hurt. Just about burst. Whereas the younger one he says it's actually truer for the older one. He feels like twaddling away but pulls himself together. Two sentences to choose from. The woman's back is music. Rejected. The music is the woman's back. That'll do.

He opens his eyes. He'd like to keep working with the kid. To send him off on an adventure he doesn't know if it sensed anything. Why should the kid just keep standing there in the corridor. Why should the kid just keep rubbing his forehead raw on this door. Why doesn't he get a running start and try to break down the door headfirst. The old man hears the splintering wood sees a kid's head surfacing out of a sea of plywood. But unfortunately the attempt fails. On the floor in front of the door lies the dead kid the fly doubled up. So another kid gets a running start.

A third a seventh. Soon a mountain of dead kids is blocking the door. You can't even see it anymore let alone break it down. So a man comes with a shovel and shovels the kiddy snow the coal heap of flies the defiantwrinklypotatoes into the basement. Then he batters down the door with the iron shovel. Smacks the woman at the grand piano on the head with the shovel. Rams the shovel again and again between the keys. Raises the shovel over his head and lets it crash down on the strings. Puts a boot on the shovel paddle poses for a picture that someone else made of someone else. Time to tidy up. The woman's hair is held in place on the side with a comb. Brown horn comb brown tortoiseshell comb. The old man tries to pull the comb out of the woman's hair. But what happened to the kid he asks.

To be as flesh. To be as music. To be as flesh music. The old man pulls a pocketknife out of his coat pocket opens it up rips open his coat stares at his earthy flesh. Old black thigh he hums and digs around in it with the blade. No pain no resistance. Fields. His thigh starts dripping though. Blackly drips the old man's flesh upon the earth. Should knell but doesn't knell. The flesh fluid refuses to be transformed into music. Soon he thinks there will be soundless bones sitting there on the bench dressed in a coat and hat. Unless the old man successfully cuts a kid out of his thigh. Rosy kid flesh that survived surrounded by necrotic geezer flesh. Like a living bullet from a pistol he hums.

Digging and digging. Until the knife melts too and drips blackly out of his hand.

Maybe a kid is much too much. Maybe a pinhead-small flesh ball would be enough. To house the old man in a point that isn't a point but as small as it is still is an extended thing. An ensouled little ball. Dwarf ball body breathing in swelling up breathing out shrinking in which sensations ball up. Which isn't only thought of but thinks. Which isn't only imagined by others but imagines itself to itself. Which composes out of its own imagination and its own thoughts its own world in which it rolls around with the sensations that roll around in it. No no. He didn't imagine what he wanted to imagine. Forgot the wide open gaping pinhead mouth pinhead anus. The peeping cells hearing cells sniffing cells cuddle cells on the pinhead scalp. The world the pinhead rolls through no pinhead would have been able to conceive of. O it's not certain that it rolls. Maybe it's squatting in a chink in the wall stuck fast in a crack in the floorboards. Waiting for another pinhead to roll up the wall to roll over the floor sometime. One so completely different that no pinhead would have been able to conceive of it. The event that would occur if through an inexplicable coincidence the second pinhead were to roll over the first one the old man calls friction. The heat that would be generated if pinhead scalp were to rub against pinhead scalp the old man calls lust. Maybe the lusty heat would be so hot that pinhead and pinhead would begin to give

off a red glow. Would soon burn out go out. Just two
little balls of flesh coal left. Two putrid black balls
of flesh coal or just one. What once were two tiny
balls of flesh might melt down to a single tiny ball of
coal. The old man pulls a box of matches out of his
coat pocket takes a matchstick out of the box lights
it takes a second matchstick out of the box holds the
burning head of the first one up against the not yet
burning head of the second matchstick what's going
to happen the second matchstick lights up the first
one ignited it two matchsticks one flame the old man
blows them out holds the first matchstick up lets go of
the second one what's going to happen it doesn't fall to
the floor it's melted together with fused with the first
one two matchsticks a single charred matchstick head
QED why should what's true for matchstick heads not
be true for combustible flesh pinheads the old man
throws the matchstick pair the matchstick dyad the
Siamese matchstick in the trashcan puts the matchbox
back in his coat pocket. The event that would occur if
the second pinhead weren't to roll over the first one
but were to roll right up next to it and just lie there
the old man calls touching. Flesh ball skin touching
flesh ball skin and being touched by flesh ball skin.
Oh the intimately nestled pinhead cheeks up against
one another. No no. Out of the question. Not even a
freak chance could bring about such a thing. No one
will ever touch the pinhead. It can turn black for all
anyone cares. It can rot away in its floorboard crack.

That does it. He curses. He's had enough of flesh balls fecal sticks maggots worms points. Why doesn't the old man reminisce about human beings. Doesn't he know what a human being is.

Eyes closed. The kid stares hard at the floor. In a triumphant circular movement the man's big toe rubs the imaginary grease stain into the carpet. The enemy mashed underfoot then squashed under a house slipper is wiped off the face of the earth. The man's gaze affirms with disdain nothing more to see down there. The word for this man is father. The foot isn't bare. It's a heel in a gray sock that's peeking out of the slipper. The toe is not to be seen but wait that doesn't work. The old man imagines the kid slipping into the grease stain disappearing into the carpet. The kid has no body but didn't lose his sight along with his body. From down there in the carpet the kid watches without fear as the naked mountain of flesh called a toe comes down on him and rolls back and forth over him. Is it possible to crush sight. The old man doesn't know should he doubt it.

Once upon a time there was a concrete tower. For many years he just stood around without even thinking about it. He wasn't particularly happy about standing there but it also didn't really bother him. Until one day he noticed that he was completely gray. How he noticed this and why after all those years of just-standingaround this gray suddenly bothered him is

not known. He probably fell in love with a toweress
that also happened to be just standing around and that
disapproved of him because he was so gray that she
fell in love not with him but with another less gray
concrete tower that also just happened to be standing
around in this region that apparently suffered no lack
of towers. It is not known with what color the concrete toweress was able to arouse the love of the gray
as well as of the less gray concrete tower or above all
with what color the less gray tower trumped the gray
tower. It was probably a beguiling pale and tender
shimmering rosy red she lured him with while the
less gray concrete tower impressed her with a passion-
ately blazing ember red. It's not even certain about this
loving tower couple that one is dealing with a concrete
tower and a concrete toweress. There are even recur-
ring doubts about whether the towers were satisfied
with just standing around and being in love. Maybe
love made little wooden wheels grow out of the crim-
son red wooden tower and enabled him to roll over
to his glimmering wooden toweress and to foppishly
wiggle waggle around her on his lacquered wheels. The
concrete tower when he noticed he was completely
gray had some painters come and soon he shone forth
a shiny red that was possibly dampened possibly inten-
sified by his hopeless love for the concrete toweress.
Years went by. The concrete tower just stood around.
From the moment he was red everything was completely different from before. Because now he thought
it was a joy just to stand around. If only it hadn't always

rained. If only the rain hadn't washed away the nice red from his tower concrete. One day the tower noticed he was gray. O it's meaningless to try to decide if he was gray once again or still gray like always. It was probably the painters who pulled a fast elephantine gray one on the tower. Instead of punishing them by taking them in his elephantine tower trunk and smashing them headfirst on the rocky ground or dumping them in the buckets with the wrong color so as to drown them in their own swindle their brew of lies the gray concrete tower preferred to believe in the passionate red in the painful red and let himself be convinced of it. Now he just stood around as he had for so many years. From the moment he learned he was gray everything was completely different from before. Because now he thought that it was a disgrace just to stand around like he did. Years went by. The awareness of this disgrace faded with the years. It didn't bother him just to stand around like that but it also didn't make him particularly happy. The concrete tower didn't know how old concrete towers could get. One day he noticed however that he had sprung a crack. It was a capillary crack but before long there were four nine sixteen then two hundred and fifty-six capillary cracks. Maybe the gray was a sign of old age the gray tower thought. Then he who his whole life long had thought about very little thought about the capillary cracks. It's incredible he thought how little even ten thousand cracks change concrete tower existence. Presumably this was due he thought to the fact that the cracks were so capillarious.

So capillarious he thought that anyone who designated them as capillary wouldn't have been far off. Since thinking about things caused him some trouble the gray concrete tower ceased thinking about things for a moment. Soon he would he knew collapse. A good opportunity to think up a few questions that because there was never any time he would otherwise never have thought about. Who built the tower and for what. Whom did he protect whom did he threaten whom did he harbor whom did he imprison he the gray concrete tower. Incredible how little the existence of the concrete tower would have changed if it had turned out that he had never been one. A gray wasp's nest tower never inhabited by a swarm of wasps has caved in on itself. A gray cardboard tower softened by the rain has fallen in on itself. Gray dust tower. Mirage. Bench and hat and herringbone coat. No old man in there.

Half time. No no. The concrete tower story needs a different ending. The tower collapsed. The ruins have just been standing around grayly for years. Then a passerby happens to pass by. He bends down over the debris pulls out his lorgnette and notices something no one else has noticed. In the gray concrete dust lies the kid shriveled up gray and small as a wasp. The passerby pulls out his notebook. Everything that's now dead he notes was once alive. Make this sentence fertile. The old man sees apple tree branches with an apple attached. Three apple trees stood in a row. Nothing to hold onto on the trunk that's far too tall. But the fourth one the small one the crippled one decried as deformed grew up against the embankment that it also grew out of so the kid could climb down into the tree. Now he's sitting in the tree house shaped like a boat. Stretching his arms. With mud on his shoes. Even if the old man squints it wasn't an apple tree.

His kid his wife. They probably left him because he could never remember their names. Because he never got that they were talking to him when they called him by his name. Because whenever he tried to touch them he missed and wound up reaching into the empty past. Cheek he says closes his eyes tries to see two cheeks nuzzled up against each other in the dark. A kid's a woman's cheek. There is he says nothing in the world except these two cheeks. Everything else is banished from the world. One of the cheeks is his he says and tries to touch the woman's cheek with the kid's cheek. To distract himself he murmurs the words lickticklescratchfuck. Gnashashwhip. Sweatingapart. Can he feel the blond fuzz he sees in front of him on the woman's cheek. Once by the lake in the mountains he was in the grass and peered over squinting for hours or minutes at the blond fuzz on the hollow of a girl's back who was lying on an air mattress in the grass or bobbing in the water. Blond hip skin. The old man's gray tongue crawls it's a gray snail over the man's gray lips and leaves behind a quick-to-dry slimy trail it's a slobber trail. The eyes get closer and closer to the cheek. When one has eyes in one's head can what one

sees touch one's cheek skin. He breathes heavily lets
out a sighing sound lays his hand on his cheek. Tan-
talus oh Twantalus oh Querulentwaddlantalus. Why
is he fooling around on the bench instead of sneak-
ing into the cheek. Again. He peers over at the pair
of cheeks and tries to use the word cheek to place
one of the cheeks on his cheek. The kid the woman
isn't it enough just to see their cheeks. To pull out the
straight razor and cut their cheeks out of the world.
No no. Is it possible to summon up something that's
not there just by looking or maybe stuttering. Can
something that's not there possibly be summoned by
feeling. Something one's never not even once sensed
can he summon it up by sensing it some day to love to
suffer as consolation as consternation. WellwhyNOT.
WellWHYnot. Who amputated the woman's the kid's
cheeks cut them off his body. He shouts the shout is
meant to say cheek but just says old man shouting on
bench. There was never a cheek there. But the fact
that there isn't one there he says and he doesn't believe
what he says and wants to believe it hurts just as if he
had just touched it. Phantom cut into phantom flesh
bliss. Overnight the cheeks have fluttered off all the
faces he's ever seen. Hunkered down up high somewhere on branches power lines antennas. The old man
tilts his head back. Keep talking pstpst. Abandoned by
all the good flesh these jaws and cheekbones just wait
around for Christmas. Maybe it will hail bloody nug-
gets o maybe it will snow muscle flakes maybe on New
Year's there will be nerve cell drifts oh a skin storm.

Maybe when it's spring teeth will start to sprout and bones will bloom. You shrub you thug the old scarecrow's eyes nearly pop out of his head enraged. But he isn't even done with the cheek story yet. Cheekchirping. Cheektrail. Southwards presumably. He always lies himself home.

And then because he's hungry or to distract himself with a game he bites the third joint off his left pinkie gnaws it down to the bone slimy berry bits tough tip inedible nail fishes the nail off his tongue flicks it in the trashcan spits out the licked-clean bone onto the ground in front of the bench. And then because his hunger doesn't let up and the game's just begun he bites the third joint off his left ring finger gnaws it down to the bone a few more berry bits just as slimy a bit more of a tip just as tough the nail a bit bigger just as inedible fishes the nail off his tongue flicks it in the trashcan spits out the licked-clean bone a little to the left or right of the other one on the ground in front of the bench. And then because nothing gets an appetite going like eating and the game's slowly starting to take off he bites off the third joint of his left middle finger gnaws it down to the bone a few more berry bits just as slimy a bit smaller or bigger or the same sized tip in any case just as tough a bit more or a bit less or the same amount of nail in any case just as inedible fishes the nail off his tongue flicks it in the trashcan spits out the licked-clean bone a little bit behind or a little bit in front of the first and second

bones on the ground in front of the bench. And then
his appetite lets up and the game's starting to get boring he bites off the third joint of his left index finger
gnaws it down to the bone how many berry bits it
doesn't matter slimy very slimy or not that slimy how
much tip who cares tough very tough or even tough-
er than that how much nail that's enough already
absolutely inedible fishes the nail off his tongue even
though he could just as well have chewed on it for a
little while longer flicks it since it seems to be a pre-
scribed move in a tedious game into the trashcan spits
out the licked-clean bone what's he supposed to do
swallow it somewhere in the middle of the first and
second and third bones on the ground in front of the
bench. And then but this is it he says because much as
he'd like to he won't be able to keep any more down
and he's bored to death with this game he bites off the
second joint of his left thumb gnaws it down to the
bone what an effort many more berry bits so what and
slimy so what and much more tip so what and tough
and a much bigger nail so what and inedible so what
and fishes the nail off his tongue for the last time
thankgod his mood's improving flicks it in the trashcan for the last time how does it go from here his
mood's worsening spits out the licked-clean bone just
like the first and the second and the third and the
fourth that's it that was it game over on the ground in
front of the bench. And then he says he would have
had to had he not decided that he was full and that the
game was over decide whether to bite off the second

joint from his left pinkie or the third joint from his right pinkie and then he says he would have had to either bite off the second joint of his left ring and middle and index finger and the first joint of his right thumb one after the other or the third joint of his right ring and middle and index finger and the second joint of his right thumb one after the other and how then he asks is he supposed to after he bites the third joint off his right index finger and the second joint off his right thumb fish his right index fingernail and right thumbnail off his tongue and then somehow flick it in the trashcan impossible impossible but even then he says this terrible game wouldn't be over instead the next thing he'd have to decide would be whether to bite off the second joint of his right pinkie and ring and middle and index fingers and the first joint of his right thumb one after the other or the first joint of his left pinkie and ring and middle and index fingers one after the other but what would happen in that case with the thumb the thumb only has two joints and both joints of his left thumb had already been bitten off licked clean and spat out on the ground in front of the bench would he have had to take the bone to which in the good old days the first joint of the left thumb was attached and rip it out of his hand bite it out of his hand or what would he have had to take all the bones one after the other to which once in darkest prehistoric times the first joints of the fingers of the left the right hand were attached and rip them out of the right hand bite them out of the left hand but even then he said this terrible game wouldn't be over instead he'd then have to decide after all the bones in his hands had been bitten off gnawed down to the bone licked clean and spit out on the ground in front of the bench whether to first take on his forearms or his feet but how then could he have bitten off on the one hand the third joint of his left pinkie and ring and middle and index toes and the second joint of his left big toe or on the other hand the third joint of his right pinkie and ring and middle and index toes and the second joint of his right big toe he hadn't forgotten after all that his feet were tucked into gray socks and gray shoes and the hands with which he would have had to undo the shoelaces had already been bitten off gnawed down licked clean and spit out on the ground in front of the bench impossible impossible unless his feet had been tucked into gray socks and gray slippers so that he could have slipped the slipper off his gray-socked and gray-slippered right foot with his gray-socked and gray-slippered left foot and then slipped the slipper off his gray-socked and gray-slippered left foot with his deslippered gray-socked right foot and then the sock from the deslippered gray-socked right foot with his deslippered gray-socked left foot and then the sock from his deslippered gray-socked left foot with his deslippered desocked right foot so that nothing would be left that could have stopped him from taking on the grand total of twenty-eight joints of his grand total of ten toes of his grand total of two feet except maybe his clumsiness because he would have had to lower his

mouth down to his toes or raise his toes up to his
mouth o he would have if he had tried to grab his toes
with his teeth on the ground in front of the bench
fallen on the ground in front of the bench o presumably he would have broken his neck in his grabbing
attempt in his fall o he would have needed his hands
his fingers to hoist up his feet to stick his toes between
his teeth o but they would have already been bitten off
gnawed down licked clean and spit out on the ground
in front of the bench o but a compromise would have
been possible his mouth his feet his toes his teeth
could have met halfway he could have without calling
on his hands crossed his legs his right leg with his right
foot on top of his left knee or his left leg with his left
foot on top of his right knee and then without falling
off the bench lunged down with his mouth at his foot
all ready at knee height that would have been possible
but even then he says this terrible game wouldn't have
been over because if he had taken his feet first he
would have had to take on his forearms next or vice
versa or his lower legs and then his upper legs or first
his upper arms but wait that doesn't work the old man
watches as his mouth feeds its way up his thigh to his
hip up his arm to his shoulder but wait that doesn't
work he wouldn't even make it to the elbow with his
teeth the knee perhaps but just barely the knee but
then that would be it but then his bite-happy snout's
culinary tour would reach its natural end he would
because his mouth would never ever make it to his
upper thigh never ever have rippedbittengnawed-

suckedslurpeddevoured the gray upper thigh flesh
from his gray upper thigh bone never ever there are
limits he says but he wasn't completely finished with
the game after all with his snout that would've even if
it had to jump out of his head and his head had to
jump off his neck tried to bite a piece out of his torso
out of his chest out of his hip out of his back in vain
in vain at the most he would have been able to bite off
his lower lip his upper lip the inside of his left of his
right cheek at the most he'd have been able to bite off
his tongue it is he says impossible to bite off everything oneself to gnaw oneself down to nothing to lick
oneself completely clean to swallow oneself without
leaving anything behind or even just to flick oneself
into the trashcan or to spit oneself out in front of
oneself on the ground in front of the bench. And then
he says good thing he only imagined all that good
thing in reality he ended the game in time bit off
gnawed down licked clean and spit out on the ground
in front of the bench only the third joint of his left
pinkie and ring and middle and index fingers and only
the second joint of his left thumb. And then out of
the five bones on the ground in front of the bench
why after all shouldn't the game keep going without
him five giants sprouted up. And then he just waits
for the pinkie giant the ring giant the middle giant the
index giant and the thumb giant to jump him knock
his hat off his head rip off his herringbone coat tear
his shoes his socks off his feet and when he's completely naked sink their giant teeth into the flesh of

his neck into his thigh shoulder back into the flesh of
his prick and devour him completely because he says
wagging pedantically in the air his proofreader's right
index finger that isn't missing a single joint it may be
impossible for one person to devour himself all by
himself but it's anything but impossible for someone
who sits by himself on a bench so he can reminisce
about his childhood to be devoured by five others who
may be hungry or may be seeking to divert him with
a game. And then it's a giant disappointment for him
that the five of them don't even take notice of him
instead the thumb giant turns to the ring giant who it
turns out is really a ring giantess and gives him or
rather her a sloppy lick-lecherous kiss on her fleshy lips
the index and the middle giant who it turns out is really a middle giantess stand side by side cheek to cheek
nuzzled up against one another in the field with love
in their eyes peering at the muted golden red sun setting in the January sky the pinkie giant who is bitterly
disappointed since neither the thumb giant nor the
index giant and above all neither the ring giantess nor
the middle giantess takes notice of him above all however that far and wide there's no sign of a pinkie
giantess with whom he if he got up the courage to flirt
could flirt so he gets back at everyone for everything
by turning his back on the old man on his bench instead of taking notice of him and either to distract
himself with a game or just because he's hungry bites
off the third joint of his left pinkie gnaws it down
berry bits pretty slimy tip pretty tough and well pret-

ty inedible nail and then of course there's the question
of what to do with the nail but the pinkie giant could
supposing a giant trashcan has already been set out for
this reason flick it into the giant trashcan and then he
could supposing that he has taken a seat on the giant
bench hopefully set out for this purpose spit the licked-
clean bone on the giant ground in front of the giant
bench andthenandthenandthenandthen biteaslongash-
ecan. And then he waits for the story to come to an
end with this digression because eventually he says
even the sloppiest most lick-lecherous kiss on the
fleshiest lips gets kissed out and no matter how mut-
edly golden red a setting sun is eventually it sets and
eventually even the smallest of pinkie giants with the
most vengeful appetite for himself either reaches his
goal and swallows himself up or learns his natural
limits and gets worn out and then he says finally it's
time again and the thumb giant and the ring giant
lurch over to the trashcan and fish out the clumps that
once were the old man's left thumbnail and left ring
fingernail and use the clumps to beat their kissed-raw
heads to death to death and the index giant and the
middle giant lurch over to the trashcan fish out the
two lances that were once the old man's left index fingernail and the left middle fingernail and stab each
other with their lances through their love-raw hearts
to death to death and the pinkie giant somersaults and
lands by the trashcan fishes out the pincer that once
was the old man's left pinkie fingernail uses the pincer
to pinch off everything his teeth couldn't reach balls

prick elbows nipples ears nose chin eyebrows eyelids
he pinches his teeth out of his mouth but he shouldn't
he says wagging threateningly his proofreader's right
finger that he seems to have left attached just for this
reason use the word pinch he snaps the teeth out of
his mouth he squeezes his eyes out of their sockets he
rips his brain out of his skull he keeps pinching away
brainlessly but wait that doesn't work o that works
alright pinching his hated-raw head to death but how
then and with what is he this torso of a pinkie giant
supposed to have held the pincer now it's quiet. And
then he feels a giant disappointment again because
that's how it was supposed to happen but that's not
what's happening because instead of fulfilling the old
man's wishes and getting rid of each other the five
giants in fact join forces the thumb giant wraps his
arm around the index giant's shoulder and the index
giant wraps his arm around the middle giantess and
the middle giantess wraps her arm around the ring
giantess and even the pinkie giant is suddenly taken
notice of what a surprise the ring giantess wraps her
arm around his shoulder a team a true team made up
of five giants what a pleasure a family a true giant
family of five only no one notices the old man on the
bench the five giants turn their five giant backs on him
their five giant icy shoulders no there are ten of them
no there's one only one of the ten giant shoulders
that's cold because nine of the ten giant shoulders are
getting warmed up by the four giant arms wrapped
around them no eight the ninth what's going on with

the ninth the old man wonders if a shoulder might possibly get warmed up by having the arm that's attached to it wrapped around another shoulder if and only if this is the case then the thumb giant's right shoulder wouldn't be cold since he's wrapped his right arm around the index giant's shoulder but the tenth one what about the tenth one the thumb giant's left shoulder is cold since he hasn't wrapped his left arm around any giant's shoulder nor has any giant wrapped any arm around his shoulder around his shoulders that should say since if anyone wraps any arm around anyone's shoulder then in reality he must have done so around both shoulders they must form a circle he sputters between his intact proofreader teeth in his proofreader mouth a giant circle so that the right corner giant of the family the pinkie giant can put his arm around the shoulder of the left corner giant of the group the thumb giant in this and only in this case none of the ten giant shoulders would be cold and yet and yet none of the giants notice the old man they should all he hissed bash each other's heads in with their giant heads they can drop dead but they aren't dropping at all not dead not alive they aren't bashing each other's heads in they aren't even in a circle they're leaving they're just leaving together it doesn't seem to bother the thumb giant that no one's put his arm around his shoulder it seems to be enough for him to put his arm around the index giant's shoulder it doesn't seem to bother the pinkie giant that he hasn't put his arm around anyone's shoulder it seems to be enough for him that the ring giantess put her arm around his shoulder they're leaving through the fields shoulder to shoulder five joyful giants why aren't they using so goes the scolding from the bench behind them the path the old man takes to the bench in the morning takes home in the evening why are they trampling across the fields they're getting smaller they're not turning around now they're as big as regular people would be if they weren't so far away the only thing missing now is their breaking out into song in a language he's never heard overjoyed at having gotten rid of the old man that too he can rot they're thinking he thinks no it's January they're hoping he'll freeze on his bench or what do we care he can bite something else off whatever he wants but probably they don't even wish that upon him they probably aren't even thinking that about him they probably aren't thinking about him at all whataboutthen wheretothen are the five giants going who are having such an unspeakably unbearably good time and now he really shouldn't start feeling like Moses just because he lets five characters he thought up go somewhere where he himself is not permitted to go. And then he takes a look at his fingers but only his left fingers and of course they've grown back so the old man is whole again and the giants are gone too and now may he please go home.

He knows it's nothing. Was nothing is nothing. Nothing will ever become of it. Not even two months left. He's not changing. Hasn't gotten a day older a day

younger. Time may have but he hasn't. He succeeds neither in reminiscing nor in not reminiscing. Can't make
a story out of it can't not make a story out of it. Nothing
hurts him. He twaddles away every kind of pain. Sits
there grins away claims it's a sad grin takes that claim
back claims not to grin takes that claim back too claims
to be grinning about not knowing first whether he's
grinning second whether if he is grinning it's a sad grin
or a not sad grin third whether he's grinning about not
knowing whether he is grinning and if he is grinning
then if it's sad or not sad but wait that doesn't work be
quiet. Getting closer. Maybe cheek would have touched
cheek if the language film had failed to form in the
millimeter-narrow interstice between the cheeks in the
moment right before right in the moment of touching.
Now he claims no if cheek had touched cheek then
the language film would have torn. Now he's got a
grin on his face inspiration he proposes substituting
the phrase letter net for the phrase language film. Bank
holdup. The letter net stocking pulled over the skull.
Who trips up whom who holds up whom. The word
skin. The word woman. The head condom that spalls
off never spalls off when one cheek nuzzles up against
another. He imagines his left cheek fluttering away to
the left rounding the globe fluttering up on the right
laying itself on top of his right cheek. Film net condom
that's all forgotten now. Not as tender as the touch of
another cheek but more tender than the touch of no
cheek at all he says. If not that now he's grinning just
as the left cheek flutters away to the left the right cheek

flutters away to the right so that the cheeks supposing that they flutter with the same speed touch on the other side of the globe just where the bench on the other side is. Unless one cheek gets caught in a storm that the other cheek doesn't get caught in be quiet. Would he the old man on the bench feel it though he asks if they his cheeks touched each other on the other side of the globe. Since they're only touching each other so that he can feel it when they touch can he conclude that he'll feel it. Otherwise they wouldn't need to touch each other at all he says but does that prove anything. Now he imagines his cheeks going astray missing one another. On the other side of the globe they flutter right by each other. Rounding the globe fluttering simultaneously up against his head the left one coming up on the right the right one coming up on the left. For a moment both of them believe the flight around the globe was in vain. Where the left one hopes to find the right one and the right one the left one there's no cheek. There's absolutely nothing a cheek would want to nestle up against. The cheek's shudder on its approach to the cheekless head. And then the moment in which they seemed to have missed each other but find each other after all. Laterally reversed but that doesn't matter honey. From the right his left cheek from the left his right cheek fluttering into a mouth. The old man's mouth. Wide open. Aren't there teeth there he says that his cheeks will have to fight their way through. They'll nestle up against one another on his tongue. If he keeps himself from biting down.

Maybe he's gay. Maybe he's perched on the bench because the bench is a boy wench a bwench. His old back is taking a rest perhaps on a bwench a boy's chest turned to wood. His old ass is it a lad's lap turned to wood that he's slipping and sliding around on. Without ever finding the peace and quiet he hoped for and abhorred. Only the herringbone coat protects him from this lad's green-skinned wood flesh. Did he in order to camouflage the fact that he's gay turn the ring giant into a giantess. He tries to imagine the thumb giant grabbing the ring giant bending over him pressing a sloppy kiss on his fleshy lips. Gag. He doesn't want to imagine that. But he wants to force himself to imagine what he doesn't want to imagine. But as soon as he notices he's being forced to do something he twaddles away. The ring giant gets a stuffed animal as a present from the thumb giant as soon as the kiss is over. The thumb giant's lips are fleshy not the ring giant's lips. What the lips of the ring giant are like no one knows except the thumb giant but no one can ask him since he's not around. The ring giant is in reality not a ring giant but a dwarf. Is the ring dwarf gay or not no one knows and especially not the thumb dwarf he doesn't exist. The creation of a lick-lecherous thumb dwarf kissing his way through the dwarf world was abstained from ok. It's bad enough that the thumb giant is pursuing the ring dwarf in the coal cellar. The old man doesn't exist either but he's still perched on that bench and says the ring dwarf on the little bench in the cellar says maybe gay maybe ungay.

Bedwetting. Diaper piss. Why did he tear out the white rubber pants' seam with his teeth. Why did he gnaw on the bumps the white bubbles in the rubber towel under the molleton. Fingernail toenail biting. Rubber pants. Sometimes pink sometimes light blue sometimes white. Soft. Memory of the taste of rubber. Plastic pants. Pus colors. Stiff. Memory of the smell of piss. While the plastic pants' rubber elastic band cut sharply into leg flesh sharply into belly flesh the rubber pants' rubber elastic band nestled up tenderly against belly flesh tenderly against leg flesh. Later on the little proofreader trimmed the pubic hair stubble that had just been trimmed a little while back. The eyeglass earpiece is deployed in the nostril when it's stuffed up. The fever thermometer is used to scratch the measles crust from the eyebrows. Even the chunks of callus broken off his heel with the nail scissors must be thoroughly chewed before being swallowed. Then he's hanging head down with one foot high up on the toilet tank hanging from the ceiling in the bathroom amazed by goose bumps and semen. The tool please the belt thank you old anxiety acrobat. It's all about the tool when there's a cheek to be had use a cheek when the cheek supply's exhausted switch to diapers. Once an olive-gray pus stick grew out of his arm. Once someone popped a mustard-yellow pus stick out of his arm. The kind of pus that pussed around in him just to pus out of him doesn't exist in this world. He consisted of nothing but pus so he consisted of nothing after the pus was gone. He sniffled. Demand a list of all the equipment that as his life flowed away out of him he stuck up the ass of his childhood adolescence manhood old age. Verify the list do not sign if erroneous. Or if incomplete. Now he's dreaming of something. Someone put the old man's head in a wet diaper. What if there's frost tonight. Everything's frozen solid. How is the old man supposed to lift his gray diaper hat.

When time's up the men from the sanitation department show up right on time. He doesn't have to stand up they just unscrew the bench. Carry it away and dump him in the bushes at an opportune moment. That's where the men from the sanitation department find him one day. He doesn't have to get up they just shovel him onto the flatbed of the trash transport truck. Drive him away and dump him on the street at an opportune moment. That's where the men from the sanitation department find him one day. He doesn't have to get up they just throw him into the dumpster on the side of the road. Leave him standing there and then at an opportune moment dump him on the sidewalk. That's where the men from the sanitation department find him one day. He doesn't have to get up they just drag him by his feet to the intersection with the major road. Leave him lying there dump him at an opportune moment TOUGH LUCK nothing to dump him in. And whatever became of the bench whatever became of the gray hat. The gray hat was left lying there perhaps in the bushes perhaps on the street perhaps in the dumpster perhaps on the sidewalk oh it's on the sidewalk. That's where the men from the sanitation department find it one day. Hey look a gray hat says the first guy the second guy picks it up the third not exactly the type to mull things over is all ready to toss it in the dumpster when the fourth guy takes it out of his hand and carries it over to the intersection with the major road where the fifth guy a polite person puts it on the old man's head. He doesn't have to get up they just let him lie there but please whatever happened to the bench. On the same day the old man was dumped into the bushes the bench was broken down by the men from the sanitation department into exactly the same pieces out of which it was assembled a little while ago a long long time ago by a notoriously thanatophobic erotophile believed to frequent sanitation department circles. On the very same day the bench parts were packaged up the boxes sent back on the very same day to the person who originally sent the bench a gentleman whose name is known to no one. Since the gentleman doesn't know the boxes are for him since his name isn't on there furthermore since the man seems to waste so much time sitting on a bench that no one's ever seen reminiscing about a childhood no one ever lived through that no time remains for opening boxes that no one ever ordered the boxes just sit there unopened in front of his door. That's where the men from the sanitation department find them one day. Hey look boxes says the first guy and the second guy intellectually average but of a dexterity not untouched by virtuosity opens them up the

third guy is already at it stuffing wood shavings bench
parts entire boxes into the trashcans that are also just
sitting there in front of the door when the fourth guy
a man who knows what he wants takes not the boxes
not the sawdust but the bench parts out of his hands
and throws them onto the flatbed of the trash transport truck where the fifth guy always polite but also
quite bright quickly assembles a bench green and
wooden a park bench unfortunately there was no park
in the boxes but nevertheless the fifth guy out of the
five men from the sanitation department his name by
the way is Jude considers for a moment whether he
should sit down on the bench and reminisce about his
childhood but then he dismisses the thought why
should a spry sixtysomething like him play a dodder-
ing geezer sitting around all the livelong day on a
bench wasting his brainpower fishing kiddie caca out
of the time toilet NO SIR but please what will happen
to the bench now. No problem for the men from the
sanitation department. They just drive to the tram stop
and dump it onto the tracks at an opportune moment.
The old man is still lying on the intersection with the
major road. That's where the men from the sanitation
department find him one day. Hey look an old man
wearing a hat says the first guy a spry twentysome-
thing with the gift of gab who doesn't mince words
his name is Jack by the way and the second guy his
name is Jeff by the way props up the old man the hat
falls off his head in the process the old man's not Jeff's
Jeff isn't wearing a hat but what happens with the hat's

no problem for Jeff we are already familiar with the adroitness of Jeff's hands while it's still in the air falling Jeff a spry thirtysomething catches the hat and the third guy is already at it about to heave the old man along with his hat into the container full of deicing sand that WHAT LUCK is also sitting around at the major intersection a man of action this third guy a spry fortysomething his name is Jim by the way then the fourth guy takes the old man along with his hat out of the hands of the third guy a blessing a gift from heaven to the sanitation department this goal-oriented decisive spry fiftysomething his name is Joe by the way and lays the old man down on the flatbed of the trash transport truck where the fifth guy we already know him good old Jude only five more weeks till retirement quite bright and always polite takes the gray hat that Joe handed up to him and puts it on well does it have to be good old Jude out of all of them who takes the hat away from the old man and who puts it on his own head NO SIR but now what is to become of the old man please. No problem for the men from the sanitation department. They'll just drive him to the tram stop and dump him onto the tracks at an opportune moment. Change of scenery no no change of scenery necessary. The bench is already there is still there. In the course of time in front of the bench a kilometer-long tram queue has formed. Traffic downtown has as they say come to a halt. Hey look my bench says the old man and gets up and stands his bench upright. It's not lying across the tracks now it's upright on the tracks. The old man takes a seat and tries to reminisce about his childhood. The trams all these trams he says but he can't think of anything. He closes his eyes. Once he was in a tram that was called a streetcar with two boys who wanted to beat him up. One of the two was from Nuremberg. Did the boys manage to beat him up he doesn't remember. He's scared to get off because then the two boys will also get off and beat him up. Lots of people in the tram among them two boys one of the two is from Nuremberg. They want to beat him up but he might just think that. He's standing up in the tram and he's scared. Maybe they got off somewhere and he stayed on. Maybe he got off somewhere and they stayed on. Maybe he got off somewhere and they got off too and maybe beat him up maybe didn't beat him up. He can't remember. He remembers he's standing up in the tram and he's scared. Maybe they never got off maybe he never got off maybe they're still riding in the tram he's still scared. It's so easy to say all that Mama. The word headlock. Put in a head-lock. Once he rode the tram and made faces and tried not to make faces and had a blue parka on that had a brown fur collar and was called a wind coat. Twice he rode in the tram once with two boys who wanted to put him in a headlock one of the two was from Nurem-berg once alone making faces or struggling not to make faces or cowardly capitulating in the struggle against making faces. He opens his eyes. The trams all these trams they've all stopped. The bench and him on it they stopped all the trams. Time passes. The bench and him on it they don't stop time. In the tram there's a tram driver compartment in which there is a tram driver his name is Hans by the way in time there is no time driver compartment so there's also no time driver he would be called Herbert by the way if he existed. Go ahead and twaddle soon everything will have been twaddled out. Instead of running over the bench lying across the tracks with the tram instead of running over the bench set up across the tracks with the old man sitting on it the tram driver Hans decided to stop in front of the man and the bench. Old Hans sits on his tram driver seat and tries to reminisce about his childhood. The bench the old men he says but nothing occurs to him. Old Hans closes his eyes. Once in the mountains he was sitting with a boy on a bench on the edge of a cliff. He was scared but he doesn't remember anymore about what. Maybe he was scared of falling off the cliff. Maybe he was scared the boy would fall off the cliff. Maybe he was scared the boy would push him off the cliff. Maybe he was scared he'd push the boy off the cliff. Maybe they're still sitting on the bench he's still scared. Old Hans opens his eyes. Time passes. Old Hans stares into the old man's eyes from above the old man stares into old Hans's eyes from below. From below on the bench from above out of the tram driver compartment. The two of them recognize each other too bad they don't recognize each other. Time passes and with time the trams pass by. The green paint is already peeling off the wagons are already rusted through there's already a whistling in the windows smashed by the bludgeoning of time who could it be the wind. Funny. The old man resolves to consider the relation of glass and time. Time passes and with time the trams fade away and in the trams tram drivers ticket collectors passengers fade away. Everyone ages. Everyone's hair turns white falls out o there are differences. One person's hair turns white but doesn't fall out. Another person's hair doesn't turn white but falls out. A third person's hair turns white and then falls out. A fourth person's hair. The old man gently places his finger on his lips. Oh Mama wouldn't it be nice if a person could just sit there in the middle of all the hair that fell out on him and see in the end the ground around him turning white. After all their hearts have stopped the fourth person's the third person's the second person's the first person's everyone is dead. Even old Hans. It wouldn't be permissible to make an exception for old Hans. O if only he had enough time enough desire the old man could tell a story about each and every tram driver ticket collector passenger. But these days there aren't any ticket collectors honey. But once there were ticket collectors. With a uniform with ticket pads with hole punchers with a little box over their shoulders with a cashier's box where the coins clattered in on the top and clattered out on the bottom with a thumb that let the coins clatter out the bottom with a heart if there hadn't been a heart beating in the chest of the ticket collector who was called a conductor his name was Heinz by the way he can't stop that naming then the man wouldn't have

been alive. Unfortunately Heinz's heart stopped later
on. Since no one brought time to a stop time brought
Heinz's heart to a stop. The agreement is one of the
two heart or time has to stop. And if the old man told
a hundred thousand stories he would not be able to
keep the hundred thousandth story from ending. It's
over. Done. Passenger onezerozerozerozerozero's
heart stopped. Just like old Hans's heart you know ok.
Grandpa is dead Mama said and then he cried. She sat
down on his bed something terrible she said has happened. On that day he got Grandpa's golden pocket
watch. Grandpa's picture had always hung next to his
bed. On that day he hid another a color photo behind
the picture. He's sitting on the rock high up above
Grandpa and Grandma. Jumping over the rock. Everyone made it over except him. Didn't make it over
the next time either. Later Grandma too was dead one
day. He didn't cry that time. At night where during the
day Grandpa's picture hung he scratched off the wall-
paper and bored his hole in the wall. Later he had to
keep boring into another wall in another house. Was
Grandpa's picture still hanging there covering the hole
he doesn't remember. The old man stares down old
Hans who's dead so he can't stare back. The old man
sits on the bench on the tracks. That's where the men
from the sanitation department find him one day. He
doesn't need to stand up they just hoist him up along
with the bench onto the flatbed of the trash transport
truck. They just drive bench man hat away and dump
the three of them into the bushes at an opportune

moment. That's where the men from the sanitation department find them one day. Hey look a gray hat a bench and on top of it all an old man Jack says. Jeff pulls the old man out of the bushes stands the bench up pats the dust off the hat. Jim is ready about to tow bench man hat into the creek. Joe takes the hat and the old man and the bench out of his hand and sets the old man on the bench and sets the bench up in front of the bushes. While Jude puts the hat Joe reached out and gave him on the old man's head. NO SIR says old Jude just as an old habit. And now please what will become of the old man on the bench. No problem for the men from the sanitation department. They just carry him on the bench to the place between forest and field to the place in front of the bushes on the path where not so long ago where a long long time ago an old man was kidnapped by a notoriously thanatophobic erotophile believed to frequent sanitation department circles. Screw the bank down and dump him at an opportune moment into childhood. Funny he says. But what if time is up.

Five weeks left. Five weeks is a long time. It's conceivable that what one person manages to get done in five weeks someone else couldn't do in five months. An old man surely doesn't need more than five weeks on a bench to reminisce about a childhood. Any old childhood. No one ever said anything about a deadline. Maybe it's smart to talk about the beginning at the end. There's no reason why the bench the old man's gotten used to should have disappeared all of a sudden from the side of the path there's no reason why the old man the old man's gotten used to should have disappeared all of a sudden from the bench.

His kid his wife. They probably died. First the kid then of grief over the kid's death the wife. He didn't die otherwise he wouldn't be sitting on this bench. Neither of grief over the kid's death nor of grief over the wife's death. The kid probably died of grief over the fact that if he were to die the old man wouldn't die of grief over it. And what if the old man had died. Then the old man probably would have died again of grief over his own death.

If his heart stops he says he'll twaddle on then no one will notice.

The interviewer. The old man often played with the idea of having him sent over to the bench but then gave up on him showing up. Now he's shown up squeezes in next to him on the bench pushes up against him butts his head up against him sticks the microphone up to his lips. Never has a mouth exhaled such an exorbitantly foul stench as the interviewer's mouth the old man says. Who would even want to know that that's not even what the interviewer asked him about. After your birth the interviewer says dates facts first year. The old man harrumphs. After he fell he says onto the tiled floor of the delivery room he just waited

to see what would happen. It's common for a man a
woman to come by and introduce themselves as father
as mother as delivery nurse and pick up what's fallen
from the ceiling. No one came. Above the delivery
room there vaulted the cloche also known as the celestial dome. Emblazoned on it were stars but they were
eyes. Even the flesh balls rolling around everywhere
another time were really eyes. While the flesh balls
were eyes that had gone blind the eyes emblazoned
in the sky still saw. He was being watched. He wasn't
ever left alone. It was known that had he been left
alone he would have died. It's not common practice
to let what has fallen on the tile floor die. The effect
a muffled sound. The cause the interviewer licking
the microphone clean. He was fed remotely watered
remotely it was seen to that the temperature in the
delivery room remained stable. Lukewarm remote
spring the whole year he wasn't cold. He didn't sweat
he was cleaned remotely. They didn't leave him without music. Iwaknotha hahbe lealo musihwha die. The
effect interviewer licking finger bones. The cause the
interviewer letting loose on the microphone with his
fist and boxing his knuckles bloody. Muffled sound is
the effect the effect only it didn't come about. It could
be thinks the old man that the microphone was shut
off before interviewer let loose. No one touched him
but on the screen installed in the delivery room for
him images were shown of cheeks lips hands with
which he would have been touched had he been permitted to be touched. If he hadn't seen those images

this much was known he would have died. Piano music was played for him. He wasn't touched but through the loudspeaker installed in the delivery room for him the reasons why he wasn't permitted to be touched were listed in the breaks in the piano music. It had to be that way he would have died otherwise. The voice that came around in the loudspeaker sometimes he called it the male sometimes the female voice. The male voice's yelling was superseded by the piano music which was superseded by the female voice's whispering. If he were to be picked up and held in someone's hand so went the yelling the fingers of that someone's hand would turn into a fist around him and he would be crushed before the year was up since that someone is so strong. Musicmusic. If someone were to pick him up and hold him in their arms so went the whisper that someone would drop him and he would be broken to pieces before the year was up since that someone is so clumsy. Musicmusic. If someone were to give him a kiss on the head so went the yelling his head would disappear in that someone's mouth and his head would be bitten off before the year was up since that someone is so wrathful. Musicmusic. He would be if someone were to tickle his stomach so went the whispering seduced into doing terrible things and he would turn gay before the year is up since that someone is so lonely. The effect a muffled clicking noise. The cause is interviewer turned on microphone that was turned off before the punch because knuckle licking was over because no more blood. The old man says nothing.

Never has a mouth exhaled such an exorbitantly foul stench as the old man's mouth the interviewer says. Who would even want to know that. The old man didn't even ask him anything. The interviewer jumps off the bench throws the microphone into the trash-can scratches his balls the old man who would like to be like him in some way also tries to scratch his balls fumbles around underneath the herringbone coat finds nothing the interviewer is gone went jogging.

Figure out then eliminate the difference between grandfather and grandpa between grandmother and grandma between mother father papa mama. Eliminate then figure out the difference between the old man telling stories about the old man and the old man about whom stories are being told by the old man. Neither figure out nor eliminate the difference between the old man and mamafa and papamo and grandmofa and grandfamo. Book two. What was in it. Don't want to know.

Once he was lying on the ground in front of the garden gate. Eventually the girl's mother came out of the house and asked how he was doing. He politely said goodbye and went home without being damaged in any way.

It's not true at all he says that childhood only grows up to be threetwoone year old.

Years after they met years before they fell out of touch he put his arm around her in the movie theater. Onetwo days later he got a card from her with her commentary on the incident that was so evenhanded so judicious so conclusive that everything remained the same and that the years in which they already knew each other could proceed without delay from the years in which they saw each other all the time.

If it has to be he rants then make it a GIANT garden gnome please.

That's boring. For an hour or a minute they waited for the streetcar or the bus without saying a word or moving. Then she took twothree steps into the street or over to the schedule to check on whether and when the bus or streetcar was coming. That's when he exploded but of course not literally. Afterwards he or she was the first to apologize that made it easier afterwards for her or him to apologize too. Afterwards he accompanied her home in the streetcar or in the bus that came of course after another hour or another minute.

He kissed Gwendolyn. His first kiss. Nicenice. That's when Gwendolyn asked what he was thinking about. Her first words after his first kiss. Nicenice. That's when he said he's thinking about how nice it is Gwendolyn and he know each other and are kissing one another. His first words after his first kiss. O phooeyeww that was a lie he wasn't thinking about anything. The young proofreader's duty would have been to say he wasn't thinking about anything. Gwendolyn's forcing him to lie was something he couldn't forgive her for. A few minutes go by and he fell out of touch with her. He's shy she said. Nicenice. What she's like he didn't say. When was that anyway. Quick say a few words. Ugly mark kidney spot big dark ears. Don't be stupid don't ruin it. Yeah should the young proofreader have whispered in her hair what Gwendolyn could see in her pocket mirror anyway. It was just a few minutes ago that he met a girl who was christened Gwendolyn after many years.

Piss off the woman on the corner said when he asked if she was waiting for someone. So he asked another one. I have to pee she said and climbed on top of the sink. It was the first time. If he had had a childhood he could have told himself stories about maybe he would have ended it right there. Perhaps fifty perhaps thirty marks. If you're used to doing it yourself you'll never get it up.

The first time. In Grandma's wing chair. He was naked. The apartment was empty. Grandma wasn't dead just not there. He had permission to watch television. He had his right foot in his hand. For a long time his heel was always his tool. When it started to come out he tried to run to the bathroom but it all fell onto the rug. Did he first start using his hand after Grandma died he couldn't remember.

Barren sentences.

Shudder. With the tip of her tongue Klaus said his sister touched his tongue. Shudder. The family on the bus. Husband wife girl all three of them licking the same ice cream cone. It went from hand to hand from mouth to mouth. So that into the shiny shrinking scoop was mixed the shimmering of three salivas.

Klaus's scorn as the promised furniture truck with the ant king's gifts didn't show up.

Addendum delivery room interview loudspeaker voice female. Musicmusic. Were they to stroke his cheek they would never stroke his cheek as well as the career strokers would later stroke his cheeks and before the year is up he would have choked on his own yawns they were such boring strokers. Scene change. A few years later. Would they take someone so young she said she didn't actually know.

Since time is up he quickly tries to act as if there had been something like a childhood.

He entered the bedroom. His father snatched the blanket and pulled it over his stomach and hands. But he saw he was all red down there. He came in to bring him a plate of apple turnovers and chocolate. He entered the bedroom. His mother rubbed the sleep out of her eyes. Not exactly handsome but a decent chap. He came in to bring her some tea or a pill.

Uncle Emil had a Chevrolet. Now that's a sentence.

A ae ae am. He won't divulge the girl's name. The shame the dwarf's gigantic shame. He had to tweak the first letter a bit to fit it into the foreign alphabet. Using a pen to enter it in the right place in the Lilliputian dictionary. The small f with a dot for the feminine. No without a dot. Between what words he's not going to say.

When time is up the bench and him sitting on it will sink into the springtime mud.

The old man pulls a slip of paper out of his pocket. That's when he thinks of the soda that's when he thinks of the bag of pretzels. He curses and asks while he's cursing if the fact that he's cursing is a life sign. Who's he asks himself cursing whom gnash no no it's him. To whom is he trying to prove he shouts that the phantasm comes to life when it downs soda when it nibbles on crispbread when it pours beer down its phantom gullet. Life's breath he shouts not chow please. More fired up by his own shouting than he ever dreamed possible he squeezes the slip of paper between his knees throws the pretzel bag three yummy pretzels he sighs into the trashcan flings the soda bottle a good liter of bubbly water he's ranting onto the path out into the fields. Does the bottle remain intact does it shatter in a hundred thousand pieces on the frozen February floe well who even wants to know that. Where the giants once disappeared now the bottle has disappeared. Basta. The old man wonders if he might have let himself get carried away and committed an imprudent act. What if he suddenly gets hungry what if he suddenly gets thirsty. That's when he thinks of the baker that's when he thinks of the grocery store. To whom is he trying to prove he shouts that the phantasm set a phantom foot even once in a grocery store. A baker's shop a beer comptoir a crispbread cellar. Risible huckster he shouts abominable phantom. If he had waited just a little bit longer if he had waited to fling the soda bottle until three days before the very last day he might have died of thirst successfully and punctually to the minute on the evening of the third day the very last day. Yeah well he should have thought of that earlier right. And does he even know if the three days estimated for dying of thirst should be calculated using the ninehourworkday or the twentyfourvegetativenohumannophantasmday or an incalculable mélange of both types of days. Now you blubber bubble-blowing blubber bubble it's too late. Now it's no pretzels no soda twaddling on day after day until it's over.

No chow. No things any more. No space. Abstract existence in time. Herringbone coat hat scarf shoes and bench he'd like to keep those though.

The slip of paper. The edictal slip prescription slip he stuck in the old man's pocket. He pulls it out from between his knees and reads what he's supposed to atone for. Assonances alliteration anaphora forbidden. Repetitions of any sort forbidden. Genitals the word and the things ballsackpricktitscunt along with procedures of any sort with these same fuckinglickingsqueezingbeating forbidden. Excessive violence burningscaldingdrinkingtodeathtrampling forbidden. Excrements shitpiss and related matters snotpukebooger ditto. Expletives of any sort forbidden. Interjections oahohphooeypssteww forbidden. Sucking on sounds sucking on syllables singsong prattle forbidden. Blubbering twaddling chitchatting gabbing forbidden. Ass the word and the thing and anacoluthon the thing alone is forbidden. Neologisms puns if they're not supported by the context this gives pause to the old man perplexed and vexed and grunts and blitzes and fizzes nonsense ellipsis soundslime sentenceslush riddlerattling all forbidden. Should he to avoid punishment tear to tatters the legal slip. No way he'll make this his last will and testament. When time's up he'll stick it to his forehead with spit so that whoever finds him will also find the slip of paper and know what child and child's child shall receive in the name of bloody he swuhswahswehswears it.

It would never occur to anyone who heard the old man that evening after evening he still hobbles home morning after morning he still sets out for his bench.

That's also not how things are. House or bench one of the two he's given up. It's not permitted he says to force someone who is always in the same place to confess he's commuting between two places. Either he no longer leaves home the kitchen table the bed or no longer leaves the bench. Fundamental decision from long ago. That's how the dice fell long ago. Just as he was felled long ago. Intermission. Moment for thought. Moment for reminiscences. He's lying on the operating table. End of moment for thought. One morning before he left the house a little before ten to eight he threw a lit match into the paper bag room so that when it was time for him to leave the bench right at five o'clock that evening according to schedule he could still see smoke rising in the near distance which indicated to him and only to him that from now on he would also have to spend his nights outside on the bench. Nota bene without soda without pretzels without beer. Hack among hacks. Here the temptation has been resisted to work in some comments about the fire department's performance presumably a conspiracy hatched in cahoots with the men from the sanitation department but the opportunity has also been passed up to denounce the conspiracy construct as a conspiracy lie after the fact. The old man sits sad on the bench. He lost his house he lost track of the plot. He wishes it would snow is that too much to ask of a mid-February day. Why didn't he when the house was still standing take his own life in the room above the kitchen that once was called the nursery. Night after night he got up on the kiddie stool and fastened the rope onto the hook in the ceiling. Hour after hour he waited with his head in the noose. If only someone had knocked on the nursery door o he would have jumped right then and there. There was never a knock no one ever gave him a chance to jump. And he's not that stupid anymore that he would hang himself without anyone watching you'll get a coin for that. Snow if it started to fall the old man would soon disappear into the landscape. Fitting it into the foreign alphabet. Snow so the proofreader explained to the apprentice whose face reminded him of the proofreader as he bored his index finger into his foolish forehead right above the root of his nose snow constitutes before all else the essence of old men in which the old man can vanish in accordance with his nature's concept and merge with it. No it's not snow that melts brat it's the contradiction of the old man and his surroundings that melts in the snow. Before snow fell the old man and his surroundings just sat around completely separate one from the other he in it and it all around him. If you have to think of something then think for example of the concrete tower. And then try to get your head around it synthesis no it's more than non c'est plus que ça reconciliation. Snow dome formerly known as old man. Sorry but that doesn't work. If snow were to fall the old man wouldn't see it falling. He'd like to but he just can't. Never has he even if he ever was a kid seen flakes tumbling to the ground woe white erratic gentle in the wind you know. Falling snow just didn't interest him. And falling flakes that little Hans didn't see big Hans won't be describing to you remember that. So it's better if he just forgets it and February goes on without any snow.

Maybe an old man is much too much. Maybe an eyeball high up in a wall would be enough. No eyelid no sleep. But also nothing to see. But it would know that down below the ground is teeming and it just can't see it.

Hit me operate on me pleaseplease don't hurt me.

Maybe nothing hurts him except everything and he just can't feel the difference anymore.

If he knew what he was awakening from what he was awakening to then he would if he were sleeping be happy to wake up if he were awake he'd be happy to fall asleep but not like this from this to this if you know what he means.

Rubbish idealist rubbish. A few blows to the face now that he feels.

He only has language he says. Not true. Language has him. Hates him.

Think once instead of twaddling too late.

Five days left. Five days is a long time. Since the house
burned down he could reminisce about the photo he
hid away many years ago on the third floor or in the
basement. An old man doesn't need more than five
days to reminisce about some photo someone took of
his childhood. Someone something bothers him about
that word. Maybe it was a self-timer. Self-timer something made him get into that word. If he himself had
been a self-timer he wouldn't have needed a mother
or father at all. The photo shows the photo showed
before it burned up in the along with the house a man
a kid a woman. The man is leaning over towards the
kid sitting on the potty on the little stool and the woman's arms are reaching out for him. The man's smiling
at the woman who even though there's no reason to
smile is smiling at the kid. The kid is smiling back the
old man is pressing his teeth together letting hot air
go through hissing into the late February day. Why he
curses doesn't this brat have guts enough to refuse to
make stupid kiddie grins. The man has a mustache and
looks like Claudio Arrau. He once saw a photo of this
Claudio Arrau on a record cover. What this Arrau was
supposed to have played he doesn't remember. Maybe
the mustache of the man in the photo is in reality the
mustache of Claudio Arrau. A café fiddler perhaps the
woman in the photo isn't even smiling at the kid but
at the café fiddler. Simultaneous smiling at two people
is impossible. Staring at two people yes smiling at two
people no honey. If someone is smiling simultaneously at two people then he's not smiling. The woman has

a skirt on with white polka dots. If it were a color photo and not a black and white photo then it would be a red skirt with white polka dots. There's no way he could know that but he knows it. The woman's hair is pinned up on the side with a comb. The woman looks like a friendly English governess. He doesn't know what a friendly English governess looks like he never had one. He also if he remembers correctly has never seen a photo of a friendly English governess on a record cover. And how could he have who even knows if governesses English or not friendly or not can sing. And even if they could sing isn't it completely improbable that there would be a gramophone record of governess-singing. That would just top things off if just because there's a friendly English governess singing that automatically a record would be made of it. That would just top things off if just because there's an ex-proofreader as unfriendly as possible and as un-English as possible twaddling away on his bench that there automatically would be a note taken in a notebook. He wouldn't have had anything against meeting the friendly English governess or the café fiddler Arrau or even both of them. But unfortunately they were burnt up in the basement or on the third floor of the house that unfortunately burnt down. If he had met both of them perhaps he would have had a childhood. The finger the woman is extending in the photo looks like a beloved coddled proofreader finger. Coddled the second the old man hears that word he squints and gnashes his teeth yeah but the word coddled read squinting is cudgel. Perhaps the kid isn't smiling at the woman in the photo but at the woman's coddled proofreader finger in the photo. The coddled proofreader finger the old man interrupts himself this can't be ignored has to be constantly yelled in the ears of the blind when read squinting is cudgel. As soon as he thinks it the thought of smashing the woman's finger with the cudgel is rejected. The finger the man is extending in the photo might very well like to look like a proofreader finger but doesn't. No connoisseur of proofreader fingers not even the type whom critical intoxication leads to presumptuous capricious judgments would ever agree to officially recognize as a proofreader finger this man's finger that even in an extended position looks lackluster clueless desperate drifting. And that's exactly why the old man says lifting gleefully obdurately his gray finger the kid is smiling at the woman in the photo's proofreader finger the coddled one and doesn't waste a second looking at the man in the photo's finger strutting around like a peacock as if it were a proofreader finger. All that's not so hard to follow if you think about it reasonably for a second. The fact that a governess finger makes a good proofreader finger and a café fiddler finger doesn't who's going to be surprised about that. In the picture a finger can also be seen attached to the kid's hand. It's not pointing at the man nor at the woman it's not pointing at anything. If everything goes well it'll become a proofreader finger if everything goes south a café fiddler finger. But it's strange the old man says that the English governess always shuts herself in to play the piano no one has ever heard ever seen the café fiddler pick up an instrument. He doesn't know how to play one the old man screeches the café fiddler Arrau can't even play the recorder. Don't lose your composure old chum pull yourself together with some geometry. If one were to pencil in some lines and connect the tips of the woman's the kid's the man's right index fingers one would wind up with an acute triangle. That's supposing the lines show up on the glossy paper. This triangle's angle sum exactly like the angle sum of the all-time lousiest or all-time loveliest ever drawn on Earth will still be does anyone know the old man raises his hand snaps his fingers crows one hundred and eighty degrees Mr. Becker. The triangle will never amount to anything more. The poor triangle will never be like the circle. Moon sun eye five franc coin woman's breast in a kid's drawing. With a little dot in the middle that reflects the nipple where the circle is sticking out. The old man falls asleep. He says that because he's scared that otherwise his brain will seep out of eye ear nose not to mention out of his mouth. When he wakes up the late February cold drizzly rain is running down his gray face. The kitchen table the bed would have been the correct solution. Now there's nothing he can do about it so he tries to think about the photo. The thing he still doesn't get is the absurd smiling on their three faces. Presumably he says they're scornful smiles. The man has a scornful smile on his face because he sees

the woman smiling at him and not at the kid and because he knows that no matter how many coins the
governess tosses at him she'll never be able to turn a
café fiddler into a proofreader. The woman has a scornful smile on her face because she sees that all she has
to do is extend her proofreader finger in the direction
of the kid and he doesn't even notice that she's smiling
at the man not at him and because she knows that if
she didn't have to use her governess wages to keep him
she would be one of the greatest piano players of her
time or the all-time greatest proofreader of all time
her pick. The kid has a scornful smile on his face because he sees right though the woman's scornful smile
as well as the man's scornful smile. The woman's
scornful smile he sees right in front of him while the
man's scornful smile he knows is right behind him.
However scornfully others may smile he smiles even
more scornfully. The old man ends up deciding it'd be
better to seek refuge from the cold by sleeping. When
he wakes up it's still not spring but it's stopped raining.
The photo occurs to him. It burned up. He'd like to
paint it over with Chinese white and when the Chinese
white dries he'll let the watercolor blobs flow into one
another on top of it. Childhood's colorful plumage he
says on loan from the old camouflage kit. Once he
colored a tree with crayons for his mama. It didn't have
any leaves but the branches were intertwined many
thousandfold as if they were roots. Perhaps someone
turned the tree upside down so that it grew out of the
air into the ground and bloomed underground. You'd

just have to dig a tad. Amen. Falls asleep wakes up. The late February sun breaks through the clouds. Only two days left. The photo is a forgery. He doesn't know the gentleman the lady the squirt. There was no smiling. Unless the smiling was for a fourth person. For the fourth person who only stopped by to take a picture of the café fiddler the governess the potty squatter. So he could point at the picture later yelling in their shriveled-up faces back then all three of them this is the proof were alive. Forged faked the old man screeches they never existed those vermin. The smiling is what proves they never existed. He's tired. He'd like to pull himself together with some arithmetic. But he can't remember for the life of him if he has to use the theory of the leastcommonmultiple or the theory of greatestcommondivisor to continue calculating the papafatherphotoman or the mamamotherphotowoman. Blush. Sorry Mr. Becker.

The second book. Not the fourth. Only three words. And that's it. Three per sentence. Four's too many. Two's too few. Yep that's right. Him and Gigi. Gigi and Gogo. Gogo and him. That's enough now. No Gugu necessary. Gugu'd be superfluous. Just like Gege. Go get lost. He loves Gigi. Gigi loves Gogo. Gogo loves him. That's not true. He hates Gogo. Gogo hates Gigi. Gigi hates him. That's true. Gigi loves Gege. Gigi loves Gugu. That doesn't work. Gege was aborted. Gugu was killed. Gaga is left. His name's Gaga. Oh dear dear. What a surprise. Gaga was born. Gaga grew

up. Gaga lived life. Fell in love. Gaga married Gägä.
Gaga begat Gügü. Gägä gave birth. To Gügü naturally. Gaga's the father. Well of course. You be quiet.
What about Gögö. Gögö's not wanted. Gögö was
aborted. Well of course. By Gaga's wife. You be quiet.
Gaga saw Gügü. And he remembered. Gege that is. Gigi's aborted daughter. And remembered Gugu. Gigi's
assassinated son. Daughters are aborted. Sons are assassinated. Some brief heckling. From Gaga naturally.
Gaga the murderer. It was Gaga. He killed them. First
came Gege. With a look. At Gigi's stomach. With Gaga's poisonouslookinjection. Then came Gugu. At his
daycare. Gaga strangled him. With his bare hands. But
not Gogo. And not Gigi. Yeah that's right. You got it.
Gogo he beheaded. Buried the head. Wrapped it up. In
some newspaper. In the cellar. Heated his house. With
Gogo's head. What a surprise. And Gogo's torso. He
examined it. Didn't like it. It was red. Wrapped it up.
Called for pickup. Fed to dwarffolk. And now Gigi.
Gaga's appetite's whetted. Freshens Gigi up. Removes
Gigi's clothes. Procures a barrel. Hammers nails in.
You righteous Gaga. Pronounce Gigi's verdict. Of tender age. Stark buck naked. Mr. Gaga's drooling. Into
the barrel. Gigi the witch. Beautiful evil shrew. O little
missymother. You poor lady. Mr. Gaga sobs. Barrel
departure time. Down the hill. Into the river. Drown
her quick. Mr. Gaga sighs. Gigi case closed. What
about Gägä. What about Gügü. Don't overdo it. Yeah
you Gaga. Gaga is tired. Go sleep Gaga. Gaga keeps
going. Telling the story. A fairy tale. He likes fairytales.

Gaga tells threewordsentencegagacockerelhorrortales. Who choked Gögö. The little Gögö. In Gägä's belly. Probably headabortionexecutor Gaga. Gaga murders everyone. Except for Littlegaga. Gaga's a coward. Gaga's getting old. Gaga's going gray. Grayer and grayer. Listen up Graygaga. Is Gaga dying. Is Gaga immortal. Gaga says yes. Gaga says no. You stupid Twaddlegaga. Gaga is scared. Gaga likes living. Wants to live. On his bench. Reminisces to himself. About his childhood. Gaga had one. Go ahead Gaga. Tell the story. About the nokisstrace. Parablegaga's lipstick problem. If no lips. If no lipstick. Then there's smearing. On Gaga's Gobicheeks. A nonexistent material. Noteosin notsalivadroplet notbreathmist. Oasisnegative fata Gagana. Gaga is flabbergasted. That's too much. You overdid it. Why the frown. Gaga's gray forehead. End it Gaga. Keep it short. Don't get gigantic. Stay gagantic Gaga. Short gagagraphic note. Gaga's gray dawnyears. Gaga's gray twilightyears. Gaga's gray noonyears. Gaga's proofreading past. Gaga wrote books. Two Gaga says. One about Gaga. Just titled Gaga. Great title Gaga. The old Gaga. And his fivemonthtwaddle. On the benchikins. That's his benchikins. Thank you Gaga. Good night Gaga. No wait please. There's the Gagacatalog. All his eats. All his feats. You know it. Gaga arranges ancientabsurdassamours. Gaga blabs benchbile. Gaga codes confessionalchimerachansons. Gaga dictates dwarfdramas. Gaga errs eternally. Gaga forgets frequently. Gaga grunts gagaesquely. Gaga hands Huzzhisheerringhonedhoat.

Gaga inherits incorporealicarianicecreamirritation. Gaga jubilates jeremianically. Gaga knows knothing. Gaga lingers listlessly. Gaga mimics meandering-musicians. Gaga negates nothing. Gaga oraculizes omamopapostracizoologicorphically. Gaga poops painterlypsoriaticproofreaderparablepoops. Gaga quakes qualmishly. Gaga rhymes realrubbish. Gaga slurps sillystorystrychnine. Gaga twaddles tittletat-tletatatumbtumb. Gaga umpires unwillingly. Gaga versifies vermin. Gaga waits woefully. Gaga xists xtremely. Gaga yangs yingly. Gaga zaps zaftigzatch-zlotys. The ageold man. The penultimate day. An emergency christening. He's called Gaga.

It's that time. Finally. Today's the last time he'll sit on his bench. Bitterly disappointed by undignified Gaga. He shouldn't have taken on the name he threw in the hat. No one not even Gaga wants to be copied out of his own book. Samuel Donatien Johannes. Now that's a name.

It's decided Gaga will think about death but he doesn't do it. Instead he tells the story of the man who one day knocks a fly off the windowpane with a newspaper. The dead fly on the windowsill bunched up in a ball. That's not enough Gaga. Gaga nods. He knows that. And what if the little ageold woman with thinning disheveled hair who almost disappears into the big white bed and sleeps barely having to breathe what if she reminds him of a dead fly bunched up in a ball.

No Gaga. Black dot. Tiny little nick disappearing into the white where the white's just a little bit less white. Don't exert yourself too much Gaga.

When time's up the old Gaga will be executed on the electric bench. That's tasteless. Gaga nods. He knows it. But he tries to imagine what will become of the will and testament slip will it be stuck to Gaga's forehead as contractually stipulated. Will it burn up be charred turn yellow or what. You should have done some research huh Gaga.

Why doesn't old Gaga take some time today to be sad for once. Objection from Gaga. Look the herringbone coat was never so dark. Look the mourning ribbon black and velvety around Gaga's hat. Gaga is in prophylactic mourning for Gaga. You see. Gaga's not sad Gaga.

When time's up the ants come Klaus and instead of feeding on the roll that as implausible as it may seem is still laying there in the dirt on the ground next to the bench will feed on our old Gaga. Lying there not laying there shut up now Mr. Becker.

Gaga tries to imagine time. A shot every second. Bang. Bang. Bang. Bang. Bang. If you consider that time is sitting there on the bench holding a machine gun then that's pretty slow and not really all that loud don't you think. Except that the shooting never stops Gaga.

And now you have to imagine that on the path in front of the bench where time is sitting an unimaginably long living bologna sausage is creeping by. No wonder it's alive you have to imagine that it embodies life. No don't put your hands over your ears Gaga your life too. The front tip of the sausage that's infinitely long and thus it has to be said Gaga the word tip's not really a good choice embodies the future are you following Gaga. One more thing. The angle formed by the time weapon and the lifewurst is a right angle. One more thing. In every lifewurst someone a he or a she is immured who eats his or her way out. That's that. And now listen up Gaga. Bang. Bang. Bang. Bang. Bang. While Gaga grins on stupidly time shoots five seconds off Gaga's lifewurst with the machine gun. Shot dead five seconds out of your future you damned Gaga. You come crawling up from behind in your sausage that's creeping by in front of the bench and up front time blows away the tip. Do you even know what would happen if you stuck your head out of the lifewurst now that there's nothing left there everything's all shot up. Bang Gaga. Hark after time shoots Gaga's future dead it'll shoot Gaga dead.

Five hours left. Five hours is a long time.

The Huzz that according to Gaga's book Gaga hugs shows up. How nice of Huzz that he's not leaving Gaga alone in his final hour. Backslapping handshaking mute gazes presumably. Perhaps Gaga gets up from the bench to embrace Huzz. Coat to coat herringbone coat to camelhair coat. Until one of them surely it's Gaga steals a look at his watch and remembers what time the bus is leaving. Or the streetcar. Heartfelt farewell. But Gaga doesn't let it come to that. A kick in the shins is what that Huzz gets and that sends him away howling. Because Huzz is an invention and Gaga can do without the consolation gained from the embrace of invented friends.

Gaga's soul has already left Gaga and is chatting away with him. This formulation is only used by Gaga to communicate the fact that according to Gaga's latest convictions if it's true that Gaga doesn't have a soul he did at one point have one. Perhaps before he was christened Gaga Gaga suggests. No comment from the soul.

If Gaga were suddenly to claim Gaga isn't old after all but rather let's say twenty years younger than everyone thought then everyone could claim Gaga's just saying that because he's scared of dying. If Gaga were suddenly to claim that Gaga's scared of dying then everyone could claim Gaga's just saying that so that everyone will believe that Gaga's really sitting on the green bench. All the while though everyone would say this Gaga has always hinted that he's only an invented Gaga. So don't all of a sudden come to us with all this twaddle about Gaga and being scared of dying. No matter what Gaga says as soon as he opens his mouth he's wrong. And perhaps everyone else is right and Gaga likes the word death in his mouth so much because he'd like to deflect attention from the fact that Gaga is completely unsuccessful at reminiscing about Gaga's childhood.

If there's a first kiss Gaga says then there should also be a last kiss. It would be nice if Gwendolyn could drag herself down to Gaga's bench one more time. Decrepit. With a cane. Trembly. Head tottering. Then our Gaga could go ahead and kiss her. What are you thinking about Gwendolyn heh he'd bark before wrapping his hands around her scraggly neck. Stop playing the clumsy blagueur Gaga. Gwendolyn's not coming and our Gaga doesn't want to have her over.

Does Gaga still remember when he pulled his Gagaprick out of a woman for the last time without knowing it was the last time. The girls he ordered in over the weekend at his house when the house was still standing. Yes but didn't you tell us the two of them rolled right over you the former as a canister the latter as a container. Now Gaga's insulted. Gaga doesn't say anything.

So Gaga why if you never managed to reminisce about Gaga's childhood didn't you ever try to seek refuge in the hereandnow. But Gaga doesn't even know what a bench is and what a February is. Bench parts he says AUTUMN late February day. Before a Gaga suddenly decides to do nothing but exist wide-eyedly outside on a bench he'd have to have a hundred thousand long distance conversations with bench frogs grounds photographers lighting describers field peepers. Gaga doesn't even have a telephone though so it'd be good if he'd just be quiet now.

When time's up it turns out the bench was sitting there the whole time on a steep incline without being bolted down. No sooner is that made known than the bench slides away along with the man on it named Gaga off the apron into the audience marveling at benches and Gagas. Of course then everyone jumps on the poor Gagas tears their hats off their heads rips the herringbone coats off their bodies and when they're completely naked digs their teeth into their necks thighs pricks because no one's going to go home tonight without their fill of Gaga.

Really quick before time's up and really it's not going to last much longer Gaga would like to tell the story of the man with the semen boils. It went like this. One day for completely unknown reasons the man's prick closed up so that the semen his testicles kept assiduously producing could only drain interiorly and thus distributed itself throughout his entire body. More than anywhere else it collected right on his body's surface right under the corium. So there soon began to form semen pimples semen wens semen pustules semen boils semen papules that completely covered the skin of this good man who knew not what he had. The boils itched that was the really embarrassing part. There's really no reason not to mention that. The man whose character come on Gaga admit it was a bit unstable started to scratch his say it Gaga disgusting semen boils in public and even in mixed company which of course in most cases caused his semen boils to pop and his bodily recesses which had always been ugly but up until now only optically embarrassing for the public or even for the ladies to ooze semen yes that notorious grayish white sticky fluid substance that smells like a laundry room like soap suds. Who then Gaga doesn't want to say anything more than this would hold it against the public and in particular the ladies that it was then soon suggested to this man that he should in the future avoid places of public social festive gatherings including gatherings where women might be present but not only those. And since we're on the subject Gaga continues surprised more than anyone else that he in his very last minutes appears to be pursuing a new career as an entertainer. Gaga would also really quickly like to tell the story about the man whose tears were so acidic that the cheeks they ran down were immediately eaten away by them which of course did not escape the man so he proceeded to consciously deliberately cry over other body parts hands arms thighs andsoforth and thus within a very short period of time was able to say of himself without exaggeration that he had literally cried the flesh off his bones. And in conclusion Gaga says with the transition to the conclusion already in his head Gaga would also like really quickly to tell the story of the man who sat naked on his bench and attached little packets of explosives to his body with wire in between them and when time was up he lit the fuse and then in exactly the intervals he calculated one explosive packet after the other went off and with each explosive packet one body part after the other got blown off until finally all the man's body parts in other words the whole man went up in smoke. And it's not true at all says Gaga who of course expected this objection that the explosive packet story doesn't actually go further than the acid tears story because the acid tears man at least still has his bones at the end while the explosive packet man doesn't have anything.

Unfortunately due to time considerations the scene had to be benched in which Gaga's blood flowed into the bench's arteries and Gaga himself turned to wood.

Would you like to shake your fists one more time Gaga. Hurry it up please.

Five minutes left. Five minutes is not a long time. Not even Gaga could claim that. Fast. Does something about Gaga's childhood occur to you. Once Gaga's brother was scared and let out a shout when he reached under the bench in Uncle Emil's garden and felt some white-rot fungus. Bravo Gaga. You'll get a coin for that.

Five seconds left. Bang. Bang. Bang. Bang. Bang.

And bang. He's no old man. Sentence without consequences.

Afterword to the English Edition

Urs Allemann's *The Old Man and the Bench* was first published in German in 1993. Allemann wrote the book over a five-month period while also working as the editor of the literary section of the Basel newspaper *Basler Zeitung*. He worked for the paper in the morning and, still at his desk in the newspaper office, wrote *The Old Man and the Bench* in the afternoon. Like so much experimental writing in today's Europe, *The Old Man and the Bench* was written thanks to government support, in this case with a fellowship from the Swiss government's cultural agency, Pro Helvetia. Allemann's text reflects on these conditions. "Prose. Some has to get finished or I'm finished," the old man writes, because he, too, has been "offered a contract. Everything he says is treated as if it were on paper. Everything on paper is treated as if he said it. Excellent working conditions."

The old man feels that, during the five months of his

contract, he must produce prose filled with childhood reminiscences, but instead he dwells on his immediate surroundings—his bench, his coat, his house—and on a series of mini-narratives about, for example, biting off his fingers joint by joint, a love triangle among concrete towers, and the chaste visit of two call girls. There are, however, moments when something like a childhood memory appears. In the middle of a tale about flies and maggots buzzing away in two receptacles, there is a glimpse of a scene in which a father, mother, and grandfather lean over the flies; no, the old man corrects himself, they're leaning over someone's genitals, maybe a child's. It seems clear why the old man might not want to write about this childhood. But we can't even be sure that this scene is from his life; it may be just another permutational narrative generated by the fly-and-maggot story. This hesitation is enough: the old man has succeeded in bringing the family down to the level of flies. He deflates the scene and twaddles on.

In Allemann's original subtitle, where German literary convention often has writers put the genre of their text, where we could have expected to read "A Story" or "A Novella," Allemann writes *Ein Fünfmonatsgequassel* "A Five-Month Twaddle" and directs the reader's attention to the old man's idiosyncratic, debased speech. "Ethics and aesthetics join hands to condemn empty talk," Peter Fenves writes in his study of chatter in Kierkegaard, "The basis of the condemnation and therefore the very category of 'chatter' is an implicit teleological conception of language."[1] Chatter blocks every progression toward unity, self-expression, and revelation. "What is it *to chatter*?" Kierkegaard asks before responding, "It is the annulment of the passionate disjunction between being silent and speaking."[2] In Allemann's texts, there is no opposition between silence and a speech that would reveal or hide the authenticity that silence is supposed to harbor. Instead, there's just twaddle, which is neither silence nor speech in the sense of meaningful communication. The old man can't shut up, so he can't really speak. "One who chatters presumably does chatter about something," Kierkegaard writes, "since the aim is to find something to chatter about, but this something is not something in the sense of ideality, for then one speaks" and doesn't chatter.[3]

The old man anticipates being the target of the anger and impatience that, according to Blanchot, often await twaddlers: "In truth everyone chatters, but everyone condemns chatter, the adult says to the child, you are just a chatterbox, just as the masculine says it to the feminine, the philosopher to the plain man, the politician to the philosopher. This reproach stops everything. One denounces idle speech and for it one substitutes a peremptory speech that does not speak but instead commands."[4] This denunciation has been interiorized by the old man, who understands his speech as twaddle, as *only* twaddle. He knows that there is some other kind of speech but he's not up to speaking it.

Twaddling seems to be an escape from compulsion ("As soon as he notices he's being forced to do something he twaddles away") but it doesn't even emancipate him from his memories ("He succeeds neither in reminiscing nor in not reminiscing"). It represents the old man's failure to liberate himself: "Every sentence as long as it hasn't been said promises to be the ungagging sentence but winds up as soon as it's been said he says gagging him." He chokes on his sentences because they seem to lack substance; they don't seem worth the effort of articulation, even though they always also promise some kind of freedom from insubstantiality.

Twaddling abandons ends and means, origins and goals, compulsion and liberation. Or it may be the result of having been abandoned by them. The old man's twaddling is as complex and as excremental as the "wordshit" described in Beckett's ninth *Text for Nothing*: "What variety and at the same time what monotony, how varied it is and at the same time how, what's the word, how monotonous. What agitation and at the same time what calm, what vicissitudes within what changelessness. Moments of hesitation not so much rare as frequent, if one had to choose, and soon overcome in favor of the old crux, on which at first all depends, then much, then little, then nothing. That's right, wordshit, bury me, avalanche, and let there be no more talk of any creature, nor of a world to leave, nor of a world to reach, in order to have done, with worlds, with creatures, with words, with misery, misery."[5] Twaddling fails to talk convincingly of any world to leave or to reach; it goes on about this world as the only world, the old man's limited world, which, despite everything, is not without its attractions. There are pleasurable and even beautiful, moving moments for the old man and his readers, when twaddling elicits other finite human activities, like laughter. And there is variety within the old man's monotony, as his twaddling sometimes seems to bring him to topics and terms that he would rather avoid, which makes him twaddle away even more furiously.

The old man's episodic existence is deprived of the conclusion that, according to Adorno, artworks were once entitled to. Like all modern works, Allemann's text lacks "the force that allowed the artwork, once it has confirmed its immanent determination, to end on the model of one who dies old, having led a full life. That this is denied artworks, that they can no more die than can the hunter Gracchus, is internalized by them directly as an expression of horror."[6] For Adorno, this inability to end is the result of artworks no longer being able to unify multiplicity. When "unity synthesizes, it damages what is synthesized and thus the synthesis."[7] The unifying and unified element in *The Old Man and the Bench* is the old man, and the damage is apparent. His twaddling escapes synthesis, at least in part, by simply continuing and creating ever more text. He is not so far from Adorno's example. Kafka's hunter Gracchus falls and dies pursuing a mountain goat, but the boat carrying his corpse loses its way, and he drifts along for centuries. Gracchus doesn't die and doesn't really live either; he is denied an end just as the old man is. Twaddling and twaddlers can't die natural deaths. The old man finishes only because his time is up.

PATRICK GREANEY

[1] Peter Fenves, *"Chatter": Language and History in Kierkegaard* (Stanford: Stanford University Press, 1993), 6.

[2] Søren Kierkegaard, *Two Ages: The Age of Revolution and the Present Age, A Literary Review*, trans. Howard V. Hong and Edna H. Hong (Princeton: Princeton University Press, 1978), 97, quoted in Fenves, 230.

[3] Kierkegaard, 99.

[4] Maurice Blanchot, *Friendship*, trans. Elizabeth Rottenberg (Stanford: Stanford University Press, 1997), 125.

[5] Samuel Beckett, *The Complete Short Prose 1929–1989* (New York: Grove Press, 1995), 137.

[6] Theodor Adorno, *Aesthetic Theory*, trans. Robert Hullot-Kentor (Minneapolis: University of Minnesota Press, 1997), 147.

[7] Adorno, 147.

URS ALLEMANN is the author of eight books of prose and poetry, as well as the editor of a volume of selected poetry by Robert Walser. A bilingual version of Allemann's *Babyfucker* was published in 2009, and English translations of his stories have appeared in *Conjunctions* and the *Lana Turner Journal*. He is the 2012 winner of the Heimrad Bäcker Prize, awarded annually for experimental writing in German.

PATRICK GREANEY is associate professor of German and Comparative Literature at the University of Colorado at Boulder.

⬜ Selected Dalkey Archive Titles

MICHAL AJVAZ
The Golden Age
YUZ ALESHKOVSKY
Kangaroo
FELIPE ALFAU
Chromos
Locus
IVAN ÂNGELO
The Celebration
ANTÓNIO LOBO ANTUNES
The Splendor of Portugal
JOHN ASHBERY AND JAMES
SCHUYLER
A Nest of Ninnies
ROBERT ASHLEY
Perfect Lives
DJUNA BARNES
Ladies Almanack
JOHN BARTH
Letters
DONALD BARTHELME
The King
SVETISLAV BASARA
Chinese Letter
MIQUEL BAUÇÀ
The Siege in the Room
ANDREI BITOV
Pushkin House
LOUIS PAUL BOON
Summer in Termuren
GERALD L. BRUNS
Modern Poetry and the Idea
of Language
JULIETA CAMPMPOS
The Fear of Losing Eurydice
ANNE CARSON
Eros the Bittersweet

ORLY CASTEL-BLOOM
Dolly City
LOUIS-FERDINAND CÉLINE
Rigadoon
ERIC CHEVILLARD
Demolishing Nisard
MARC CHOLODENKO
Mordechai Schamz
STANLEY ELKIN
Mrs. Ted Bliss
GUSTAVE FLAUBERT
Bouvard and Pécuchet
FORD MADOX FORD
The March of Literature
JON FOSSE
Melancholy
MAX FRISCH
I'm Not Stiller
CARLOS FUENTES
Terra Nostra
WILLIAM GADDIS
J R
The Recognitions
JANICE GALLOWAY
The Trick Is to Keep Breathing
WILLIAM H H. GASS
Cartesian Sonata and Other Novellas
JUAN GOYTISOLO
Count Julian
HENRY GREEN
Back
JOHN HAWKES
The Passion Artist
ELIZABETH HEIGHWAY, ED.
Contemporary Georgian Fiction
AIDAN HIGGINS
Bornholm Night-Ferry

Flotsam and Jetsam
Langrishe, Go Down
Scenes from a Receding Past
ALDOUS HUXLEY
Antic Hay
Crome Yellow
Point Counter Point
Those Barren Leaves
Time Must Have a Stop
GERT JONKE
Geometric Regional Novel
HUGH KENNER
Joyce's Voices
DANILO KIŠ
A Tomb for Boris Davidovich
TADEUSZ KONWICKI
A Minor Apocalypse
The Polish Complex
ALF MAC LOCHLAINN
Out of Focus
MINA LOY
Stories and Essays of Mina Loy
BEN MARCUS
The Age of Wire and String
WALLACE MARKFIELD
To an Early Grave
DAVID MARKSON
Wittgenstein's Mistress
HERMAN MELVILLE
The Confidence-Man
STEVEN MILLHAUSER
The Barnum Museum
OLIVE MOORE
Spleen
NICHOLAS MOSLEY
Accident
Hopeful Monsters
Impossible Object

FLANN O'BRIEN
At Swim-Two-Birds
The Poor Mouth
The Third Policeman
PATRIK OUREDNÍK
Europeana
BORIS PAHOR
Necropolis
MANUEL PUIG
Betrayed by Rita Hayworth
RAYMYMOND QUENEAU
Pierrot Mon Ami
ANN QUIN
Berg
ISHMAEL REED
Juice!
RAINER MARIA RILKE
The Notebooks of Malte Laurids Brigge
STIG SÆTERBAKKEN
Siamese
Self Control
KJERSTI A. SKOMSVOLD
The Faster I Walk, the Smaller I Am
GILBERT SORRENTINO
Imaginative Qualities of Actual Things
Mulligan Stew
Something Said
GERTRUDE STEIN
The Making of Americans
GONÇALO M. TAVARES
Jerusalem
JEAN-PHILIPPPPE TOUSSAINT
Television
DUMITRU TSEPENEAG
Vain Art of the Fugue
ÁLVARO URIBE AND OLIVIA
SEARS, EDS.
Best of Contemporary Mexican Fiction